A DOLLOP OF DELIGHT

A Recipe for Love Novel

KELLY COLLINS

Copyright © 2021 by Kelly Collins

No part of this publication may be reproduced, distributed, or transmitted in any form or by any means, including photocopying, recording, or other electronic or mechanical methods, without the prior written permission of the publisher, except as permitted by U.S. copyright law. For permission requests, contact kelly@authorkellycollins.com.

The story, all names, characters, and incidents portrayed in this production are fictitious. No identification with actual persons (living or deceased), places, buildings, and products is intended or should be inferred. All products or brand names are trademarks of their respective owners.

Chapter 1

Chloe Mason spun in a circle as pallets of equipment made their way into the conference room. It was looking more like a theatrical production than a hotel meeting space.

The deep hum of a table saw droned on in the distance as the production's stage crew erected walls and lighting to fit the show. Browns and pinks and creams took over the once opulent muted gold walls.

"Quite the production, right?" a voice asked from beside her.

She jumped in response and slapped her hand to her chest. "You scared me." Spinning around, she saw Todd Lundgren, the hotel's maintenance supervisor. "It's crazy how they can make an empty room look like it's been a bakery for years." She watched them unwrap the plastic wrap from each pallet to reveal workstation equipment—six pallets equaled six contestants.

She'd never watched *The Great Bake Off* until her boss asked her to oversee the setup to make sure Luxe was represented well.

"Are you the representatives from the resort?" An older woman with red glasses perched at the end of her nose rushed toward them—her squeaky voice arriving first.

Chloe smiled. "Yes, I'm Chloe, the pastry chef for Luxe." She motioned to her counterpart. "This is Todd Lundgren, the head of maintenance and engineering."

"Thank God." She pointed toward the faux wall being erected as they spoke. "Plumbing is going to be an issue. I'll need you over there."

Todd turned to Chloe, and his expression didn't require words to convey his thoughts. She had the same reaction. Were they working for Luxe or Blue Box Productions?

"And you are?" Chloe wasn't a stickler for much, but manners were important.

The woman waved her clipboard through the air. "I don't have time to play hostess of the welcome wagon. We're already behind schedule, and we've only just begun."

Chloe took a cleansing breath and tucked her hands into the pockets of her white chef jacket so she wasn't tempted to choke the woman.

"No one is asking you for tea and cakes, but it would be nice to know who we come to with questions." On the outside, she was smiling, but inside she was cussing like a sailor—a drunk sailor who'd stubbed his toe.

As if those words poked a hole in the woman's bloated persona, she deflated there on the spot.

"I'm sorry, it's just that everything that can go wrong has. My name is Hildy, and I'm the set director."

A loud crash sounded behind the wall, and words that would make a hooker blush echoed through the air.

"I think that's my cue." Todd took off toward the noise.

"What can I do to help?" She'd already worked six of her eight-hour shift and was dead on her feet. With the resort gaining popularity, occupancy was running at ninety-five percent, and with the show coming to Luxe, they were at one hundred percent capacity.

The one thing people loved to eat on vacation were sweets, and she couldn't keep up with the demand.

"You're the kitchen girl, right?"

Chloe wanted to throw her hands in the air but pointed to the embroidery on her jacket. "Pastry chef. Although, I'm a sous chef by trade."

"Sous chef? Isn't that the second-place chef?"

If she had a dollar for every time someone made her feel less, she'd be rich.

"It's not a placeholder but a career choice." Sous chef was a prestigious position in the kitchen. While the executive chef was in charge, the sous chef ran the show and the staff. In her opinion, an executive chef was only as good as his sous chef. It was like having a body and no arms. Not much would get done.

The woman tucked her clipboard to her chest and started toward the pallets. "Why anyone would settle for less baffles me. Take this contest, for example. The winner gets a hundred grand. Second place gets ten, and third, five. There's such a difference between the best and the others."

Chloe wasn't one normally driven to violence, but at that moment, she wondered if the industrial-sized trash compactor would be efficient at disposing of Hildy, whose name was perfect because it only showed up in a similar form on shows with witches. All this woman was missing was a wart on her nose and a broom.

"Not everything is about position." Why was it that lies tasted so bitter on the tongue? Who was she kidding? She'd been competitive since she was a kid. Being the second child didn't help. Being chosen for everything last wasn't an ego booster either. Her entire life, she lived in the shadow of her sister Gabby who was Luxe's sous chef. Their family was chef royalty. Her grandfather was the once-famous Fortney Mason. Her father, Michael, wore the crown when grandpa retired. The art of cooking drove her grandfather, while fame drove her father. In their culinary royal household, Gabby was the heir apparent, and Chloe was the spare. Yep, second place again. She hadn't thought about her position as a pastry chef in terms of hierarchy but imagined it would sit somewhere between court jester and serving wench.

"Did you get that?" Hildy asked.

Chloe was lost in thought. "Umm, sorry. I got distracted. What did you say?"

"I don't have time to babysit you." She pulled a paper from the back of her clipboard. "Make sure to set up the workstations the same, and I mean exactly down to the inch and ounce." She pivoted and walked away.

"Wait a minute." Her words fell on deaf ears as Hildy disappeared behind the faux wall. "I don't work for you. I have a full-time job already." She let her head fall back as she sighed. "This is going to be a long day."

"You got that right." A tall man dressed in a suit stood to her right, while a second man stood to his side.

"I'm Leo Birney, the producer." He pointed to the man on his right. "This is Ryan Cross, your host."

Not my host. She offered her hand and introduced herself. It felt more like offering her condolences. She wouldn't be caught dead competing in a show like this. After the Aspen Food Festival, she decided that she'd never again enter a contest where there was one winner, and they deemed the rest losers. At least, that was how her father viewed it. Even a tie was a loss to him.

Ryan inched around Leo and smiled at her. He was a nice-looking man, but not her type. He was the guy who'd use all her hair products and concealer.

"It's quite the production. Do you move from city to city?"

"Just this season. Until now, we had worked out of lot 36 in Hollywood Studios. Everyone came to us, but the ratings slipped, so we switched things up."

They had done so much advertising that she couldn't turn on her television without seeing a commercial for the show. She had to give it to Allie; Luxe was getting a lot of free press.

"You think location will do it for you?"

Ryan blinded her with his smile. "Sure, it's now a destination show. Who doesn't want to visit the rich and famous in Aspen?"

She laughed. "This isn't Aspen. It's Timberline."

He shrugged. "It's a sleeper community, so it's close enough."

"Right, tell that to a souffle you pull from the oven a few minutes early. Close enough never really cuts it."

A phone rang, and the producer pulled it from his pocket. "Leo here." He walked a few steps away from them.

"What's a cupcake like you doing in a place like this?" Ryan inched closer, and she resisted the urge to hurl. For someone who could have any girl he wanted, he sure had the worst pickup line. Then again, maybe because he could have any girl he wanted, he didn't have to try that hard.

She pointed to herself. "This cupcake is earning a living." She glanced at the sheet of paper in her hand. "It turns out I'm a jack-of-all-trades today. I should get working on putting the kitchens in place."

"What do you mean she broke her leg?" Leo's voice echoed through the large room. It seemed to bounce off the walls and come back at her. "Can't she work on crutches?" The producer stomped his feet and flailed at the air around him like a kid throwing a tantrum. "We don't have time to find a replacement."

Not wanting to get caught in their line of fire, Chloe put her head down and rushed toward the first pallet where she found the stagehand. "Hildy told me to set the stations up, but I can't do it alone." He seemed relieved and happily rushed to her aid.

"You mean Godzhilda?"

"Is that what you call her?"

He chuckled. "Yep, but only when she's nice."

She couldn't imagine what Hildy looked like on a bad day. They followed the layout to the inch on the page. By the time they finished, there were six identical workstations. But she had a feeling they'd be tearing one down the next day if she gleaned the correct information from Leo Birney's tone and disposition. It sounded like there was trouble in paradise. Their recipe for success was one egg short of a half dozen.

She was on her way out when she realized she'd taken her jacket off midway through her project. Turning around, she headed back to the kitchen, where Leo and Ryan leaned on a prep table. "We need a last-minute fill-in."

"Excuse me," Chloe said as she reached for her jacket.

"Hey, cupcake," Ryan smirked. "Are you hot in the kitchen?"

She rolled her eyes. "Yep, I sweat like a cow in a slaughterhouse." She painted the most unpleasant picture she could, hoping his weak attempt at flirting would fall like that souffle she told him about.

Leo frowned. "What he means is, are you an exceptional baker?"

Usually, she would have said yes, but she knew where this was going, and it wasn't anywhere she was interested in visiting. They either wanted her to be one of their eggs or find one to get them to their desired quota. She didn't have time or the desire to be either.

"We're not known for our baked goods." That wasn't exactly true. There were rave reviews online about the treats she whipped up. Though she wasn't a baker by trade, some of the best had trained her. You couldn't be a Mason and connected to La Petite Mason and La Grande Mason without knowing how to bake. The French were known for their culinary skills, but especially their baked goods. She whipped up a perfect flourless cake, and her chocolate souffle was award-winning. She could make cookies in her sleep. Quick breads were another matter. There was nothing quick about them, and hers always turned out like a brick. She was sure if she stacked them, she could build a room that not even a category five storm could blow through. Everyone had their Achilles heel—that was hers ... and cupcakes. She'd been trying out new recipes, but like her quick breads, her cupcakes were always heavy.

In the distance, she heard the staccato of Allie's heels. It wasn't every day that she wore them because she'd adopted a dressed-down approach to her job, but her walk was recognizable. It was a *clickety-clack* that reminded her of a rapid-fire weapon from a war movie. She imagined it was because Allie was all of five feet tall and had to move her feet twice as fast to keep pace with everyone else.

"Have a nice day, gentlemen." She swung her jacket over one shoulder and walked away. They'd already gotten her pound of flesh, and she had nothing more to offer. She'd rather be covered with honey and hung beneath a beehive than get involved in a baking show.

"How goes it?" Allie asked.

"It was a cakewalk." She smiled at her pun.

"I hear they are in the middle of a crisis?"

She shook her head. "I have no idea," she lied. What she professed not to know couldn't hurt her.

As she walked away, she laughed at herself. She had let her ego take over the commonsense part of her brain. That was a Mason family trait she was trying to break.

There was no way they'd ask her to compete or help find a replacement. There had to be hundreds of applicants that represented the best bakers from around the country. Surely they'd choose from those.

Chapter 2

Gage Sweet was an early riser. That habit came from his father, who clanged pans in the hallway at four in the morning. His dad ran the family, and the business, like military boot camp. As he stared at the glowing green light of his clock, waiting for the next minute to tick by, he groaned and reached for it before the four o'clock alarm went off.

"Time to get up."

Sassy stretched her long limbs and snuggled closer to him as if to say, "Just five more minutes."

He scratched the top of her head where she liked it, right behind her ears. The purring started, and he knew she'd get her five more minutes because he didn't have the heart to stop.

He'd like to say that he rescued her, but the truth was, she saved him. He came home one day and found her curled on the mat by his front door. She was a mess, with scratches marring her face and part of her tail missing. As soon as he opened the door, she strolled in like she owned the place. The funny thing was, she did. She might not pay rent or clean or do laundry, but little miss Sassy was a queen, and she knew it.

A Dollop of Delight

"Seriously, girl, you need to earn your keep. It would be great if you could at least start the coffee in the morning." He'd been trying to teach her how to press the button, but she was a cat, and they did as they pleased.

After a final scratch behind her ears, he rolled out of bed and readied himself for the day. He followed his father's routine. It was the three S's of his life: shower, shave, and shine. Sassy rubbed herself against his leg, making sure the fourth S, Sassy, was cared for before he rushed out the door to Sweet Eats.

Today he was running a little late and could hear his father's voice in his head. *"Boy, early is on time, and on time is late. Never be late. It's disrespectful to your customer and me. You disappoint me."*

He moved down the dark street and turned the corner to the family bakery—fifty years of baking Sweets. There was Albert Sweet, his grandfather. Martin Sweet, his father, and now him. Three generations of Sweet men who rose before the sun to make bread.

As soon as he entered the shop, he knew something was wrong. Call it a sixth sense, but it was like the building spoke to him, and he had that gut feeling something was off.

Then again, it could've been the water on the floor that got his attention.

"Not again." He let out a growl that would send a bear in the opposite direction. He'd been Band-Aiding the place together since his father died a year ago.

He sloshed through the water and followed the mess to its source, a leaky pipe under the sink.

"I don't have time for this." He flipped the switch to the ovens and started on the cleanup. Again, his father's voice echoed in his memory.

"You can't do anything right. Someday this will be yours, and

you better fight for it. We've got fifty years of blood, sweat, and tears invested in this bakery. It's your legacy."

"Got it, Dad."

Gage turned off the water and mopped up the mess before placing the loaves of dough he made yesterday into the proofer. There was a time when artisan bread was a thing, but it was hard to stay competitive with mass production.

He'd tried to convince his father to expand their line and include baked goods like cakes and cookies and muffins, but Martin Sweet was all about tradition, and Sweet Eats was a bakery and bakers made bread.

"Honey, are you here?"

He dumped the rye flour into the mixing bowl and pressed start.

"Hey, Mom." He wanted to laugh. Who did she think was in the back making Mrs. Borowitz's rye bread? It was Monday, and she'd be in at three to pick up the single loaf. "Who else would be here?"

For the last forty years, his mother showed up dressed like she was going to church. She didn't do any of the baking. In the Sweet family, that was man's work. Mom's work was stocking the display racks, looking pretty, and running the register. His sister Courtney Sweet was their accountant. He couldn't wait to tell her that the "As Seen on TV" pipe tape she bought to save money failed. That would go over like a pregnant pole vaulter.

"Why does it smell so musty in here?" The *tip-tap* of mom's heels sounded as she walked across the checkerboard tile to the back.

"Because I just mopped up an inch of water that leaked from the pipe below the sink."

His mom was only in her fifties, but she looked older. The years of trials and toils had taken their toll.

"Your father would be so disappointed."

Gage picked up a nearby towel and threw it across the room. "Yeah, I know, Mom. I heard about his disappointment all my life. Pleasing Dad was like petting a porcupine. It was impossible and painful."

Mom made the sign of the cross even though they weren't Catholic and said, "Don't speak of the dead in such a disrespectful way."

He shook his head and went about making the bread.

At seven o'clock, he unlocked the door and let in the regulars, who were Gerald and Wilson, two octogenarians who came for the free coffee refills and a dozen games of checkers before they paid their bill and left.

Gerald scrunched his nose as he entered. "What's that smell?"

Gage frowned. "That, my friend, is the smell of disappointment."

Wilson narrowed his eyes. "Sure, smells like mold to me."

By ten o'clock, the bakery was empty, and his mom was counting the morning income. "Slow morning." She pulled out three tens and a five. "How are we going to keep this place running if we can't pay the rent?"

"I've been telling you and Dad for years that we need to expand the line. People don't want hot cross buns and Kaiser rolls. They want muffins and cupcakes and trifle and cookies."

"That's not who we are."

The look on her face was comical to Gage. It was like a shocked emoji—enormous eyes and a mouth rounded out to a silent O.

"We can't be who we were and survive."

"What would your father say?"

He wiped his hands on his apron. "The one thing about Dad was he was never short on words."

"This is your legacy, Gage. This bakery has been in our family for five decades."

He'd heard it all before but listened to his mother drone on about responsibility and ancestral pride.

"What will Jesse do if we fail?"

"I don't know, Mom. Maybe he'll grow up and do something he wants to do. Imagine having a firefighter or veterinarian in the family. Maybe he wants to trade stocks at the Exchange. Maybe he has dreams that will never be realized because of family expectations."

He watched his mother's face fall along with her shoulders.

"Has your life been so tough?"

Not every day was terrible. He remembered his first successful loaf of bread. It was whole grain wheat that had the perfect consistency. His father stood proud and showed every customer that came into the bakery that loaf of bread. It sat on the counter for a week like a trophy, and Gage had been trying to make his father that proud ever since.

"No, Mom, I love baking, but there's more to life than bread. If this is my legacy, let me do it my way and pass on the love of the craft and not just the chore."

She rubbed the crease between her eyes. "But your father—"

"Is dead, and we have to survive. Look around you. There's no one here to save us. We have to save ourselves." He'd been surviving on a shoestring budget for years. Something had to change.

As he turned to put the next batch of bread into the oven, it flickered and groaned before it shut down.

"Not again." The damn place was falling apart, piece by piece. The old building was telling him something. It sounded like "run for your life."

Gage spent the rest of the day working on the oven but couldn't fix it. They had two ovens, but sadly, the one that went down today was the good one. The other baked unevenly and sometimes didn't bake at all. It was moody and temperamental like some women he knew.

By four o'clock, he'd given up. "Let's call it a day," he said to his mom.

"But it's not five."

He looked around the shop and saw a single loaf of bread available. He took a five from his pocket and walked to the register. "I'll take that loaf, please."

"What are you doing?" she asked.

"I'm buying the last loaf so we can go. I know you, and you won't leave until it's gone." When she didn't ring him up, he scooted around the counter and charged himself. "Tomorrow's another day."

He closed the place and walked out to find a homeless man sitting on the bench out front.

"I appreciate anything you can spare," he said.

Gage had very little, but what he had, he was willing to share, so he handed the man the loaf of bread and headed to his sister's. They needed to come up with a plan. No ovens meant no bakery. This was his legacy, a building whose trouble rose faster than the bread he baked.

Courtney paced the kitchen.

"I thought for sure that tape would give us some time."

Gage poured himself a cup of coffee and sat down at the table. The same table he'd eaten at since he could remember. The metal-ridged edge wrapped around a white speckled Formica top. Some things lasted forever, and some things weren't meant to.

"We don't need time. We need money."

Courtney stared at him and then at the stack of mail on the

table. One stood out. It was a brown and pink envelope that her eyes kept going to.

"I have a plan, but you need to be on board."

He didn't like the sound of that. The last time his sister had a plan and wanted full cooperation before divulging said plan he had gotten grounded and his ass whooped.

"I'm not stealing the Dairy Queen cow again. Who pissed you off this time?" His sister was eight years older than he was, and back then, when he was ten, she easily influenced him. Then again, he always had a soft spot for the women in his family—all women, really.

"Life pissed me off. Just say yes."

He shook his head. "No way. Not until I know what you've gotten me into." Knowing his sister, it could be anything from bank robbery to stripping for Thunder Down Under.

"Uncle Gage." Jesse ran into the house and threw himself at Gage. At ten, he was small for his age but smart as a whip.

"How's my favorite nephew?"

"I'm your only nephew."

He ruffled Jesse's hair. "I never could get anything over on you."

Jesse slid to his feet, and like his mother, he stared at the pink and brown envelope.

"Did you tell him, Mom?"

Not willing to wait for another second, Gage swiped the envelope from the table and looked at the Great Bake Off's return address.

His gut twisted.

"What did you do?"

"You're going to be on TV, and you'll win and save the bakery," Jesse said as he bounced on his sneakers.

"Oh no, I'm not." He tugged his nephew onto his knee. "Hey buddy, when you grow up, what do you want to be?" He thought he'd have to wait until Jesse ran a thousand careers through his head, but he didn't have to wait long.

"I'm going to be a baker like you and papa." He rubbed his chin. "Or a bank robber."

"A what?"

"Seriously, they have the best cars for getaways."

Gage let out a breath. "Baker it is." He glanced at his sister, then back to the letter in his hand.

Congratulations,

We have chosen you as one of six contestants to participate in this season's The Great Bake Off.

As he read the details, sweat gathered on his brow.

"I can't do this."

His sister smiled.

"Yes, you can. Besides, I already confirmed for you, so you have little choice."

"I always have a choice." The words sounded nice, but their meaning was moot. He never had a choice.

Chapter 3

Chloe tossed and turned all night, dreaming about baking contests. The last thing she remembered before waking up was the host kicking her out of the kitchen and telling her that her dessert fell flat.

"Fat chance of that. I know the difference between cornstarch and baking powder." Besides, she'd already made that mistake and swore never to do it again. It was hard to tell the ingredients apart when they were stored in unlabeled containers. One made things rise. The other made things thick. Thick, dense cake was a thing, but you didn't get it from cornstarch.

She looked around her cluttered kitchen. There must have been a dozen dry ingredients on her counter.

While she wasn't known for her neatness, she had a system that seemed to work for her. To everyone else, she appeared to be a holy mess, but it was controlled chaos. The creative side of her couldn't be set free if everything was institutionally neat. She imagined her ingredients were like a painter's palette. A little here and there and everywhere, and when she mixed them, the magic happened.

She looked at the clock and panicked. If she didn't head out now, she'd be late. Her stomach roared while she waited for the elevator. She could probably wait until she got to work. At that thought, her stomach knotted as if trying to prove how empty it was.

"Fine." She rubbed her belly. "I'll stop at the bakery." She laughed because she was having a conversation with her stomach.

When the door opened on the lobby level, she bolted outside and turned right. She'd never been to Sweet Eats, but it sounded like the kind of place a girl could get a muffin and a cup of joe.

Moving her legs double-time to make up for the detour, she nearly jogged the two blocks.

At the door, the scent of baked goods slipped through the crack.

"That smells like bread." She lifted her nose into the air and inhaled deeply. "Rye? Maybe pumpernickel?" She walked inside and looked at the half-empty display cases. Behind the counter was a woman who looked straight out of a fifties or sixties sitcom with her perfectly styled bob and her sensible checkered dress. If she could see the woman's feet, Chloe bet she'd be wearing a pair of black pumps.

"Good morning, Welcome to Sweets. What can I get you?"

"Do you have breakfast sandwiches?"

The woman shook her head. "No, but we have bread."

"I can see that. Okay, do you have muffins?"

The woman shook her head. "No, but we have bread."

Chloe stopped for a moment. She imagined her expression was one of confusion.

"I have rye and wheat." She turned toward a door behind her. "Gage, when is that sourdough going to be ready?"

A man walked out from the back room. His apron was pristine white to match his teeth. He smiled at her, but she knew that smile. It was the same one she used when she was busy, and guests at the resort wanted to talk about her lemon meringue pie.

"Sorry." He glanced at the oven as he walked forward. "Ten more minutes for the sourdough."

She cocked her head. "Um, this is Sweet Eats, right?"

"You're in the right place," he said.

"I'm looking for a muffin?"

"We don't sell them." He turned toward the older woman and gave her a stare.

"So, what do you sell?" It was a stupid question.

"We sell bread." The woman picked up a wax paper square and swiped a roll from the display case. "Try a hot cross bun. My son has the best buns."

Before Chloe could say no, she found a warm roll in her hand and her eyes trying to get a look at the baker's buns.

"Sweet Eats isn't good branding if you don't sell sweets." She didn't have time to give them a business 101 lesson. She'd already been there too long. "What do I owe you?"

"Enjoy," the woman said and walked into the back room.

"Thanks." Before Chloe could stop herself, she motioned for the baker to turn around, and to her surprise, he did. He filled out those jeans perfectly. "She's right. You've got nice buns." Feeling the heat of a blush burn her cheeks, she spun on her sneakers and raced out the door.

It took her fifteen minutes to get to her car, drive to work, and park. She clocked in just as the minute hand hit twelve.

"Pushing it to the minute, aren't we?" her sister Gabby said as she breezed past her.

Chloe lifted the half-eaten bun into the air. "I was hungry."

Her sister rolled her eyes. "You work in a restaurant." She shook her head. "I'll whip you up an omelet."

As much as she wanted to say no, she couldn't because her belly growled a definitive yes. "Bacon and cheese, please."

"And veggies," her sister called back.

Chloe liked veggies, but she liked bacon and cheese better and knew her sister would add in asparagus and mushrooms rather than bell peppers and onions.

"Hey, girl," Kinsley said from behind her.

For a woman who was with one of the wealthiest people in the area, she didn't understand why Kinsley insisted on working. Then again, she did. Women were often relegated to child-rearing, cooking, and cleaning. Their social lives were limited to play dates and accidental meetings at the grocery store. Kinsley worked to maintain a sense of self.

Chloe leaned in. "Anything I should know about?"

Having a buddy married to one of the owners gave her inside information. She enjoyed being the first to know things.

"Apparently, the show is missing a contestant, and they need to fill the spot, or the episodes won't go as planned. They are calling all the second-tier contestants right now."

A flood of relief washed through Chloe. There had been no need for her to worry. It was a silly thought that she'd have to step up and step in.

"I'm sure they'll come up with something."

Flynn, her boss, peeked his head out of his office. "Chloe, you're wanted upstairs."

"For what?" she asked.

He shrugged. "I don't know. Maybe they want to say thank you for the job you did on setting up the workstations. I heard they look great."

Everyone liked praise—those who didn't were crazy. A good thank you was almost as amazing as a kiss. Then again, it had been ages since someone had properly kissed her. She tried to remember who that was and couldn't. Working for Michael Mason left little time for a social life.

"Allie is waiting," Flynn nodded toward the elevator that would take her to the executive offices.

"Wait," her sister said, rushing forward with the omelet. "You can eat this on the way."

It was a ten-second ride to the thirteenth floor. Why they made that the executive offices, she couldn't say, but speculated that it had something to do with superstition and people not wanting to stay on the thirteenth floor.

"Thank you." She took the plate and fork her sister offered and wolfed down the omelet as fast as she could. Luck was on her side because the elevator stopped several times to let employees on and off. By the time she reached her destination, she had two bites left. She gobbled those up and put her plate in the employee lounge before heading to Allie's office.

At the closed door, she knocked gently, and a soft, "Come in," greeted her.

"You asked to see me?" Chloe walked in and stood in front of the desk.

"Yes." Allie pointed to the chair on Chloe's right. "Have a seat." She rubbed at her eyes as if she'd been up all night. The dark circles under them confirmed she hadn't slept enough.

"Am I in some kind of trouble?" She couldn't imagine what she'd done to get summoned to HR, but the woman staring at her didn't look like she was in a "thank you" mood.

Allie waved her hand through the air. "Oh, no. I heard you did an outstanding job on the setup. Thank you."

Chloe frowned. It was the thanks she wanted, but the delivery was less than exciting.

"You're welcome. It was challenging, but I was happy to help." She lifted from her chair. "Can I go then?"

Allie shook her head and sighed. "No, I need to ask another favor of you."

She sat back down and stared at Allie. "Sure, what can I do for you?"

"I need you to help the production crew again. Flynn said he could put another person on desserts so you don't get behind."

"The production crew needs me?" She thought about Hildy and wondered if her broom got her home safely the night before.

"Yes." Allie smiled, and while it looked warm and inviting, the twitch at the corner of her lip was a dead giveaway. She was forcing it, and her muscles were fighting back. "They liked the way you stepped right in and took over. They find that a good quality in a baker. I think Leo's exact words were, 'she's a fighter and goes the extra mile.'"

"Okay." That felt nice. "What's the favor?" A feeling of dread began as a prickle at the back of her neck and slowly spread like hands wrapping around her throat. "Just say it."

"Welcome to *The Great Bake Off*. We've selected you as the sixth contestant."

"Oh no. I've got a job."

Allie held up her hand. "I'm told this will only take about four hours of your day."

"I'm not a baker."

Allie raised her brows so high they disappeared under the sweep of her red bangs. "Am I mistaken? We hired you as a pastry chef. I can attest that you have baking skills. You made my Chantilly cake, and it was magnificent."

"Well, I followed a recipe. You know, I'm a sous chef with a hint of talent in the baking department. I'm not a baker, and I won't be a contestant." She rose and started for the door.

"You've been reassigned. You are a halftime pastry chef and a halftime social ambassador for Luxe. Your first assignment is to represent us in the baking challenge."

"What if I lose?" A cold sweat broke out on her forehead.

"Then you lose, but at least you tried."

Her entire body shook. "That's the thing. I don't have a losing bone in my body. I can't lose, or it will destroy me." The competition didn't drive her to win but not to lose. She was always just out of reach of first: Second favorite daughter out of two. Tied at the Aspen Food Festival with Gabby. Sous chef, because yes, Hildy was right. She was second in charge when she held that job, but her father fired her and then replaced her.

"That's a little dramatic, don't you think?"

Chloe had to agree. She was a drama queen, but maybe that was the only way to get out of this mess. "Have you watched that show?"

"Sadly, I've only caught one episode, and that was late last night. Honestly, it seemed like the perfect match for you."

Perfect match? It was like being thrown in the deep end of the pool and not knowing how to swim.

"Why would you say that?"

"On last night's episode, they threw in a savory and sweet challenge. Can you imagine using salmon in a sweet muffin? That's where you have a leg up. You're a sous chef, which means you can do anything."

"Is this negotiable?"

Allie shook her head. "No, sorry. I mean,"—she shrugged—"you can quit, but I hope you don't. I know it's an inconvenience, but honestly, they just need a body. You can throw the competition on the first round and be done."

"Didn't you hear me? If I have to compete, I'll do my best to win. I'm not a quitter."

Allie slapped the table and stood. "That's the spirit. I knew I could count on you. You Mason girls are fighters." She walked to the door and opened it. "The prize is a hundred grand, and you get bragging rights for being the best baker."

"A hundred grand?"

"Yes, the stakes are big, which is why they needed you."

Chloe's adrenaline rushed through her veins. Her brain was screaming no, but the inside mechanism that created her insatiable drive to be the best at something kicked in. They might have chosen her as the booby prize contestant, but she'd be the big prize winner.

"Okay, I'll do it. I'm not happy about it, but I'm a team player."

Allie seemed to relax. "I'll let them know. Take the next couple of days off. Competition starts in three days."

"Three days?"

"Bake their buns off." Allie walked past her and disappeared down the hallway, leaving Chloe at the door to the office.

Had she really agreed to do it? It wasn't as if she had much choice. It was compete or quit. Deep down, she knew Allie wouldn't have forced her, but she still hated that she allowed herself to be manipulated.

She made her way back to the kitchen. She had three days to bone up on her baking skills. Sure, she was the pastry chef, but that's mostly what she made. She could whip up a buttery croissant that would make a French baker cry, but her cake skills were lacking. There wasn't much demand for cakes with automation or muffins with salmon in them. Cupcakes she had down. Slap some batter into a paper cup and slather it with buttercream icing. Ask for anything fancier, and she was lost.

"I see you got the news," Flynn said.

"You knew?"

He nodded. "I couldn't tell you."

"Did Gabby know?"

He grimaced. "I hear you have the next few days off."

"I do, and I'm out of here." She marched toward the locker room. Why was she always the last to know? It was another example of never coming in first.

Since she was heading home for a few days, she took the spare clothes and uniforms from her locker with her. When she opened the door, she scrunched her nose and stepped back. Obviously, she hadn't been in here in a few days if the musty smell was an indicator.

With a swipe of her hand, she emptied the shelf. On the top of her pile of clothes was a book that she'd never seen before. She picked it up and turned it over to read the front.

"*Recipes for Love*," it read.

"You've got to be kidding." She glanced at the ceiling as if she could see through it. "Is this a joke or divine intervention?" Since she couldn't be certain, she packed the book up and took it home with her clothes.

Chapter 4

He wasn't one to throw a tantrum, but last night Gage threw a doozy. It wasn't the stomp your feet kind of fit that his nephew was famous for, but the quiet brooding he'd learned from his father.

He stuck his K-cup into the machine and pressed start. Good, strong coffee was a luxury he afforded himself each morning. Lord knew he couldn't get the buzz he needed from the diner blend his mother made. Drinking that was like drinking dirty water.

The cat slipped in and around his legs, purring all the while. He'd like to think it was affection, but she was waiting to be fed.

"Hey, Sassy girl." He leaned down and gave her a pet before doctoring up his brew. "Can you believe what she did?"

He sat last night with his finger on the dial button, ready to call the show's helpline but slept on it. No good decisions were ever made in haste. Or that's what his father taught him.

He figured he'd give it a day, and then he'd decide what to do. He pulled down a can of Pretty Kitty and popped it open.

"You hungry?"

She let out a meow that sounded more like a hairball that got stuck in her throat. He imagined her vocal cords got damaged during the battle she'd survived. She was primarily silent unless she was ravenous.

They say you should pick your pets carefully, but she didn't give him an option. Sassy chose him, and he didn't have the heart to turn her away.

He put her food down and gave her a nice scratch to her ears. "You be good," he said. "No parties." He grabbed his coffee and headed for the door. "No inviting that tomcat over either." He'd seen another stray hanging about and wondered if word got out that there was a sucker for disenfranchised pets.

As he hit the sidewalk, he took a moment to breathe in the fresh air and listen to nature come alive. Some things never got old, like the chirp of birds first thing in the morning. It was like they were taking roll call, asking each other if they made it through another night. Or maybe they were talking about worms and who filled their bird feeders with fresh seed. For all other species, their only aim was to survive.

As he made his way to the bakery, he considered his life. In many ways, he felt like a bird on a wire. Every day came with its set of challenges.

The bakery was dark as the sun peeked over the building across the street. A ray of sunshine lit up the "Sweet" on their sign. The paint cracked and peeled. Everything was falling apart.

"Morning, honey," his mother said, coming up behind him. "How did you sleep?"

"I didn't." That was partly true because he tossed and turned all night, thinking about what his sister had done to him. On the one hand, it was a blessing. If he won, which was a long shot, he'd get a hundred grand to fix up the bakery. If he lost, they were exactly where they were right now.

"You know, this is the perfect opportunity to show the world your baking chops. It's good for the bakery as well. We get free advertising."

He opened the door and walked inside, grateful that he didn't find an inch of water. Then again, he'd turned off the water before he left, so finding a lake would have meant there were bigger problems than a fractured pipe.

"I'll put the coffee on."

"Perfect." He lifted his to-go cup and took a drink of his bold brew. "We should upgrade our coffee. That's like drinking watered-down instant."

"It's what we've been serving for fifty years. What would our regulars say?"

He chuckled. "Mom, half of our regulars are edging on dementia, and the other half bring their coffee because ours is awful."

"Your father loved my coffee."

That brought a bigger laugh. "No, he didn't. He took it in the back and added a teaspoon of espresso powder. He loved you and would never want to say anything about your coffee."

His mother's jaw fell open. "I don't believe it."

"No?" He walked to the oven and flipped the switch, praying it would come on. When it did, he breathed a sigh of relief. Unfortunately, they were still working with only one oven. "When Stan comes in for the internet, offer him a cup on the house."

She crossed her arms and harrumphed. "Deal." They moved into the back room where the proofers were and pulled trays of bread from the racks to put in the oven. "Now, what are you going to do about the show?"

"You mentioned free advertising." When his mother opened her mouth to speak, he held up his hand. "Let me finish."

"Okay, honey." She smiled and leaned against the counter. "Tell me your plan."

"The advertising would be great if we sold sweets. That's been a problem all along. We have a brand discrepancy. Sweet Eats gives a vision of cupcakes and cookies and everything destined to give you cavities and heart disease. When you walk in and find only bread, it's a disappointment."

"Our bread never disappoints."

"Mom, it's not about the quality."

"It's always about the quality."

He couldn't argue, but she wasn't getting it. Mom was old-school word-of-mouth advertising, but it was a different world now. Sweet Eats had no presence outside of the local neighborhood.

"You're right. We must have quality or what's the point, but we also have to have brand loyalty, which means we need a brand. Yes, Sweet is our last name, and it makes sense to call a bakery Sweet Eats but only if you can play on the word sweet."

"You've been trying to get us to expand for years, but your father said no." She pushed off the counter and walked to the coffeepot, where she poured herself something that resembled tea. "Why fix something if it's not broken?"

Talking to her was like talking to a cinderblock. "Have you looked around lately? Everything is broken. A couple of hundred dollars in sales a day can't support three families. I'd make more working at the coffee shop down the street. My point is we have to up our game. The bread was great when you couldn't get a hundred different varieties at the grocery store. What we need is more. More of everything." He checked on the bread in the oven and let out a growl when he saw one side was browning faster than the other. He quickly turned the pan and shut the oven to continue the baking process.

"You never answered about the show."

He rubbed his chin and thought about it. Did he have much choice? It was their best chance to make changes. Then it occurred to him. It was their last chance, and he had options.

"I'll do the show, but there are conditions."

Mom gave him that raised brow look when she couldn't believe what she was hearing. "You are setting conditions?"

He nodded. "I am. I will do the show, but if I don't win, we close the bakery. We can't keep it open on a shoestring budget. Every time we turn around, something is breaking."

"She's fifty years old," she said.

"I know, and like a fifty-year-old, her joints are creaking, and things aren't the same as when she was a teen. The building needs maintenance."

"But to close it? What would—"

"My father say?" He rolled his neck and felt several pops. "Mom, he's not saying anything anymore. I run this bakery, and from now on, I'm running it the way I think it needs to be. Dad is gone, but I'm here. Sweet Eats will sell sweets along with bread. That's the only way I'm doing the show. We have to agree that if I don't win, we close the bakery, or you get someone else to run it for you. If I win, we'll upgrade everything and create a new menu that is on-brand with the name Sweet Eats." He moved from behind the counter. "I'm talking about everything new." He pointed to the walls and the floor, and the tables. "A whole fresh look like a sweet country bakery. The only thing that remains is the name."

Her hand went to cover her heart. "Oh, I don't know."

He shrugged. "Those are the terms. Take it or leave it."

She tugged at the collar of her dress. "I guess I don't have a choice."

He walked to her and pulled her in for a hug. "You know what? There's always a choice." Wasn't it just yesterday that he thought the same thing? Now he had two choices. He could go with the status quo, and nothing would change. Or he could take a chance on himself. Who better to bet on? The only person he could control in any situation was him.

He went to the front door and turned the open sign to closed. "We'll open back up in a few weeks."

"If you win," his mother said.

"I will win," he said with a false sense of bravado and confidence. How hard could it be?

Chapter 5

Chloe's hands shook, and the back of her neck prickled with sweat. The panic attack washed over her like a tidal wave, undulating and crashing until she was sure she couldn't breathe. Events like these always dragged her under the surface, and she fought to pull air into her lungs.

The contestants gathered at one end of the conference room, lifting champagne glasses and smiling as if they weren't mentally sharpening their knives for the kill.

The scene was oddly reminiscent of the Aspen Food Festival, where treachery and tyranny were the names of the game. That was the beginning of the end for her. She had a choice back then. Go for the guaranteed win and ruin her sister or even the playing field and win by skill.

"You look deep in thought," Hildy said from beside her.

Chloe leaned against the wall and watched the competitors

"I like to approach slowly. You can learn a lot from someone by watching their body language."

Hildy leaned on the wall beside her. "Tell me what you see?"

Chloe crossed her arms and narrowed her eyes toward the group.

"There are only four contestants."

She shook her head. "No, you're number five, and the sixth person hasn't shown up yet, but he will. I have it on good authority that he needs this win."

"Don't we all."

Hildy shrugged. "Some need it more than others." She nodded toward the group. "Now tell me what you see."

Chloe took in the scene. There were two men and two women. They seemed to hit all the major demographics of gender, age, and race, and she wondered if one was LGBTQ.

"The older woman seems grandmotherly."

"Don't let the gray hair fool you. Isabel is a firecracker, and she's in it to win it."

"The tall man beside her looks more like a basketball player than a baker."

"Oh, he is. That's Dwayne Washington. He used to play for the Sabers but ruined his knee, so now he's making a play in the kitchen. The tiny little cherry blossom next to him is Lilly Watanabe. She owns the bakery chain Baby Cakes."

Chloe sucked in a breath. "Those are my mother's favorites." Her heart picked up its pace. This would not be a friendly bake-off. When she looked at the four of them, there was a fire in their eyes.

She kicked off the wall. "I suppose I should meet the competition."

"It was quite nice of you to volunteer."

She faced the set director. "I didn't have a choice."

"Will you throw the first round?"

"Never. When I'm in, I'm all in. If I'm here, I intend to win."

"Good for you." She cocked her head to the side. "Make sure they don't give you the yellow or white shirts."

A Dollop of Delight

Chloe wasn't sure if Hildy was being helpful. "Why not?"

"Because white would make you see through with your white hair. Then again, maybe you want to blend into the background."

"I'm rarely one to blend." With her almost platinum hair, she never disappeared. "Why not yellow?"

"Girl, that's not your color. You need something bold like hot pink or purple. Even black would be preferable. The camera will not love you if you wear white or yellow."

"Thanks, I'll take that into consideration."

Hildy laughed. It was more a cackle and made Chloe think maybe the woman did commute to work on a broom.

"It's out of your hands. You'll be assigned a color."

A lot of things were out of her hands these days. Not a comfortable feeling.

"Who chooses?"

Hildy smiled. "I do, of course."

"So, what color am I getting?"

She put her finger to her chin. "Yellow." She walked away, laughing.

"Why are people so freaking strange?" She made her way to the group and introduced herself.

"Hello, I'm Chloe Mason, and I'll be joining you on this journey."

Lilly smiled. "Nice to meet you, Chloe. You're Michael Mason's daughter, right?"

She would've loved to deny that. Despite what she knew about her father, no one else seemed aware of his unscrupulous practices.

"I am his daughter."

"Michael Mason?" asked the young man she hadn't gotten the details on from Hildy. "That means your grandfather is Fortney Mason."

She nodded. "Yes, but he's passed." Every time she thought

about his death, she felt sick. The robbery was senseless and losing the man who taught her how to make the best chocolate souffle in the world was a loss she'd never recover from.

"I'm so sorry to hear that." He offered his hand to shake. "I'm Matthew Braddock. I'm from the great state of Texas."

"Nice to meet you." His name sounded familiar, but she couldn't place it. "What's your claim to fame?"

He waved at her in an aw-shucks way. "I'm the owner of Levity."

She wanted to toss the towel in right now. Levity was a premier bakery specializing in cakes—imagine Duff from Ace of Cakes but catering to the rich and famous like the President. She was sure if the Queen of England wanted a cake, she'd call Matthew Braddock.

Isabel cleared her throat. "Well, I'm just delighted that I get to be here to compete. An old girl like me doesn't have many rodeos left."

Chloe remembered what Hildy said, but this sweet older woman didn't seem like a firecracker.

"I'm sure you've got a few tricks up your sleeve," Dwayne added.

Matt looked beyond her. "Looks like our sixth has arrived."

Chloe turned around and couldn't believe her eyes. "Mr. Sexy Hot Cross Buns."

"Amen, sister," Matt said. "Mmm mmm mmm."

She knew right then the show had tried to fill all the demographics. The only thing missing was a child, and she wondered if maybe she was replacing a cooking prodigy.

"Hey, I know you," Gage said, staring at Chloe as he walked up.

Before he could say another word, Matt slipped a glass of champagne in his hand and sidled up beside him.

"But you don't know me, and we'll remedy that right away."

She watched the Adam's apple bob in Gage's throat. "You're Matt." He turned to the basketball player. "Dwayne Washington. I watched you help win the game against the Celtics." He glanced down toward Dwayne's legs. "That was a tough break."

"Brutal, man, but I'm happy doing what I'm doing. My red velvet is to die for, and my cookies and cream..." He kissed his fingers and opened them to the air.

He glanced down at Lilly, who couldn't have been over five feet tall. "Lilly Watanabe. It's so good to see you again."

Chloe watched him interact with the cute baker.

"Gage Sweet. What the hell have you been up to?"

Chloe took a step back. This felt like some kind of reunion, and she wasn't an alumnus. Then again, neither was Isabel, but she didn't look bothered. Maybe she was Gage's grandmother, and no one knew it. There seemed to be a connection. Gage knew who Dwayne was. He obviously had some kind of relationship with Lilly. Matt didn't seem to know him but was keen to. She was the odd man out. But was she? She'd met him last week.

"Hey, Muffin Girl," he said. "Were you scouting out the competition last week?" He lifted a brow which only made him cuter. She loved men with expressive faces. Actually, she loved men who smiled. Her father never did. So, it was an anomaly and a treat to watch a guy grin, and even though his greeting was on the snarky side, his smile showed he meant no harm.

One thing she was very good at was fighting back. She could give as good as she got.

"Competition? Really?" She laughed. "This guy runs a bakery called Sweet Eats but doesn't sell a sweet in the place."

Matt's eyes sparkled. He stepped back and took in Gage's backside. "No, but you're right. He's got nice buns."

Gage's eyes shot up, and a smile lit his face. "Is that right? Did you say that?"

"No, I said your store had great hot cross buns."

Grandma tittered. "That is what she said." She leaned and pretended to whisper, but her voice was louder than if she talked normally. "But I'm fairly certain she wasn't talking about bread."

"I most certainly was." Indignation colored every word. "His mother offered his buns, and I took one." As soon as the words were out of her mouth, she wanted to breathe them back in, but it was too late. Laughter spread like a contagion until they were all doubled over, including her.

"Looks like you're all getting along," Leo said. "That's nice because everything changes tomorrow. This is war, and at the end, only one victor will remain."

She felt like Katniss Everdeen at the Hunger Games. But instead of a bow and arrows, her weapons were a stand mixer and a spatula. Let the games begin.

"We are baking, right? I mean, I don't need a weapon."

Grandma smiled. "Sweetheart,"—she tapped her head—"this is your weapon. Arm it daily, and you'll be fine."

Leo went over the rules while they sipped their champagne. He held a bag that had workstation assignments.

Grandma chose first because she was the oldest and a girl. She chose station number three. Chloe chose one, and Lilly got five. It was like the baking gods were dividing the group into boy-girl pairs. Though no one would help the other, the person you were closest to would become almost like a roommate since you'd be sharing airspace with them.

Matt chose next and got number six. Dwayne pulled the number four, which meant Gage was her next-door neighbor.

"Hey, Muffin Girl, looks like you and I will share some secrets."

"You wish." She wiped her hands on her jeans and offered him a shake. "I'm Chloe, not Muffin Girl, and I locked all my secrets up inside."

"We'll see." He turned away but swung back around. "You can call me buns if you'd like." He chuckled.

"I'll stick to Gage, or what about Mr. Sweet?"

He winked at her, which would generally make her feel all icky. Who winked these days? She didn't know, but he had the swagger of a stripper and the eyes of a sinner. He was as delectable as a cream puff and as unpredictable as her Gramps' famous soufflé. All the other contestants were completely capable of winning the contest, but there was something about Gage Sweet that told her if she didn't keep her distance, he'd take away more than the hundred grand.

"I hate to drink and go, but some of us have to work." She put her nearly full glass of champagne on the table and waved to the group. "See you in the morning."

"Bring your A-game," Lilly said.

Chloe kind of liked and hated her at the same time. Liked because she seemed sweet, but hated because there was something about her and Gage knowing each other she wasn't keen on.

"You, too."

Lilly laughed. "I won't need my A-game. I see the competition, and it's B level at best."

Bam, there was nothing like hitting a girl's ego with a bat. Maybe it was the competitive edge kicking in. Would Gage and Lilly start an alliance and try to push everyone out so they were the last two standing?

She shook her head. This wasn't *Survivor*. However, someone was getting booted from the island soon. If she weren't careful, it would be her. Maybe this was all about surviving. Nope, it was about winning. After she frosted hundreds of cupcakes, she'd dig into a few cookbooks. That made her think of the one in her locker that she brought home last week. It had been sitting on her counter, taunting her daily, but she refused to pick it up. *Recipes for Love* was the title.

"That's not happening," she said as she walked away. She wasn't looking for love. If she had written the book and it was an autobiography, she would have called it *Chloe: A Recipe for Disaster*.

All she needed was a win that was all hers. Could she do it?

Chapter 6

A sudden surge of adrenaline pumped through his veins as the host called his name. Gage came from the sidelines like a boxer entering the weight class above him. He had this. He could win.

Everything seemed muffled as Ryan Cross brought in the other contestants. The only name he heard was Chloe's. Maybe that was because Ryan said it twice, but she appeared frozen in place on the sidelines.

Without thinking, he rushed to her and took her hand. "You've got this." He led her to her workstation and took his place beside her.

"Welcome to *The Great Bake Off*," Ryan said. He then explained the rules and how, over the next several weeks, they would eliminate contestants. One bad day didn't end it all for the baker, but the points over two competitions were added together, and the low man was out.

"Today is a sweet and savory challenge, bakers." He scanned the six contestants. "Do you play it safe or risk it all?"

Ryan pointed to a table that looked more like a breakfast buffet full of bacon and sausage and smoked salmon and capers, along with pulled pork and barbecue sauce. There were goat cheese and green olives and a myriad of other savory ingredients. On a table next to it were cotton candy and chocolate chips, honeycomb, and maple syrup hard candies. At least a dozen odd but sweet ingredients were laid out in front of them.

He glanced at Chloe and saw that all the blood had left her face. Even her hot pink shirt couldn't give her color.

"You okay there, Little Ms. Muffin?" He knew that would get her to focus, and it did. She spun around and shot flaming daggers at him.

"It's Chloe, Mr. Buns."

"Looks like the competition has already begun. Play nice in the kitchen," Ryan said. "You have one hour to create a sweet and savory muffin. You must use at least one item from each table. This isn't the time to play it safe. This is the taste round. Let's see what you've got. Your time starts now."

Gage moved like his mother at a shoe sale. He'd never seen a woman run so fast in heels as she did when Macy's put their pumps on sale.

He attacked the savory table like a hungry bear, swiping and grabbing at the ingredients he wanted. It wasn't as if he'd be locked out of anything, but the melee added to the excitement of the show.

For a moment, he was back in the Aspen Sweets Extravaganza. That's where he met Lilly. He knew right away she'd reach for the bacon because she wasn't a risk-taker. She approached food like a home décor expert, which wasn't a bad thing. She would mix nothing that didn't pair well. He reached the sweet table and handed her the maple syrup candy. She'd whip up a cinnamon muffin, add bacon, and put a cinnamon candy crumble on top.

She smiled and took what he offered. "How did you know?"

"You're predictable. Maybe you should bring that A-game, after all." The night before, he'd been disappointed at her for sniping at Chloe. He knew it was Lilly's way of getting in others' heads. She ruled by intimidation.

"Won't need it." She hugged the ingredients to her chest and walked away.

He gathered his ingredients and went back to his workstation. Chloe hadn't moved from hers.

"You going to start, or are you giving up already?"

Her lips lifted slowly into a smile. "I'm no quitter. I'm a planner." She strolled over to the table and picked up a few ingredients, one being the salmon, another being the goat cheese, and she moved to the sweets table and grabbed the cotton candy. On her way back to her workstation, she swiped up the capers. He didn't know what she was creating, but a salmon muffin would never go over well with the judges. She'd have to whip up something spectacular to pull that off.

He laid out his ingredients and worked in the same manner he always did, attacking everything with measured efficiency. He lined up everything in order of use and went to work making his standard batter while he stared at the pulled pork and barbecue sauce. At the pantry, he picked up the container labeled baking powder and grabbed the cornmeal. Today he'd make a pulled pork muffin filled with barbecue sauce and frosted in creamed corn icing.

When he got back to his station, everything had changed at Chloe's. She moved around like a madwoman. Scattered ingredients were around her table like she'd hosted a kindergarten class and gave them free rein over her work area. Flour flew in her hair as she dumped ingredients into the stand mixer and started it. Behind her, she placed the cotton candy in the pan and melted it down before adding butter and brown sugar. If he had to guess, he'd say she was making a brittle.

"Salmon is the way to go if you want to lose. No one wants a fishy muffin."

She laughed, and her cheeks pinked, which was a welcome change from the ghostly white color her face had adopted only minutes before.

The camera crew moved around them like ants at a picnic, but Chloe was in the zone and didn't seem to notice them.

"Slow starter, huh?" He mixed his cornbread batter and added some of the creamed corn to it. He shredded the pulled pork and added it to the barbecue sauce. Most people would dump it into the cups and let it bake, but he would fill the muffins after the sauce so it didn't evaporate into the muffin. Besides, filling them now would only make them look like a murder scene once the judges broke them open. Nothing looked worse than a red sauce after it had seeped into the bread.

"Slow start but a strong finish." She scooped her batter into a pan and shoved them into the oven before she went back to the stove and dumped the capers into the mixture, then carefully spooned them onto a pan lined with wax paper.

"Wow," he said. He hadn't considered candying capers, but he could see how that might bring her muffin up a level or two.

On the other side of him, Isabel worked like she had all the time in the world. She was using sausage and scrambled eggs. Her muffins looked more like a frittata. She covered the mixture with batter and drizzled maple glaze over the top.

"Sometimes simple is easily the best approach." She walked the pan to the oven and slid it inside before setting the timer for twenty minutes.

The other three contestants were out of his range of sight, so he had no idea what they were making, but the room was filled with various scents of chocolate and bacon and, right next to him, the salty brine of fish.

The clock ticked down as he went to work on his muffin topping, which was a cheesy onion crumble that he put on the warm muffins before they cooled.

A Dollop of Delight

To his right, Chloe rolled the salmon into florets and filled them with a creamed goat cheese.

He took in her workstation, which was covered in flour and bits and pieces of everything she'd used.

"Do you always work in a mess?"

She stared at her workstation and laughed. "You think this is a mess. You should be there when I have to frost hundreds of cupcakes. It's pure mayhem."

"I'd go nuts." At about the same time, all six oven timers went off, and Ryan announced they had fifteen minutes until judging. Then it was ten minutes. Then five, and all contestants frantically prepped their plates until the time ran out.

"Stop." Ryan pointed to the judges and introduced them one by one. They were a cornucopia of talent getting ready to try everyone's first entry.

"Today, we'll go by station number, starting with Chloe." She gripped the edge of the table until her knuckles blanched.

"What I've prepared for you is a lox and cream cheese bagel muffin with a toasted sesame, cream cheese frosting, and caper brittle."

The three judges peeled the paper cup away and took a bite.

Gage watched for their noses to crinkle or for them to move the bits around the plate, but every single one of them took a second bite.

The French baker cleared his throat. "Excellent," he said. When we said muffin, I never expected a bagel, but it works, and the salmon and cream cheese work too. What's amazing is the caper brittle. I could eat an entire plate of it if you let me."

The other two judges gushed over her muffin, and they moved on to him.

"What I've prepared for you is a pulled pork corn muffin with a creamed corn frosting." He smiled and looked to his right and left.

Isabel smiled her grandmotherly grin, and it felt like she was silently hugging him. Chloe watched the judges intently as they made their critique. No one gushed over his creation, but the comments were positive.

Grandma sweetened her entry with a story about her granny and how she made the breakfast muffins for her husband as he left to work in the coal mines. While the muffins got her a solid performance rating, they wouldn't get her a win.

Next up was Dwayne, who presented his cardamom goat cheese and candied fig concoction, which got him a five-star rating. Lilly went safe, and that ultimately would send her home if she didn't up her game. The judges said her muffin, while delicious, was predictable.

Matt surprised everyone with his fruity pebble muffin with brown sugar glazed cheese curd topping.

It was a toss-up who would win the first round. Gage knew it wasn't him, but he didn't think he'd be on the bottom, either.

The bakers stood while the judges deliberated. When they finished, they announced the winners.

"In first place, we have Dwayne with his fig delight. Second goes to Chloe with her caper brittle lox and bagels. In third, we have Gage with his ode to southern barbecue. Coming in fourth is Matt with his fruit and cheese muffin. Fifth is Isabel, who took the coal and buffed it to shine. In last place is Lilly."

One look at her thin lips and stiff posture, and he knew she'd bring her A-game tomorrow.

Their scores were placed on the leaderboard, and the episode ended.

"That's a wrap. See you tomorrow for day two."

Chloe started cleaning up her station.

"I thought you were going to buckle at the knees," Gage said.

She took a bite of an extra muffin she had on her table. "I should probably eat before I compete."

He shrugged because he was confident that wasn't the issue. "You want to get some coffee. I hear the shop across the street does a decent latte."

She shook her head. "Sorry, I have to work. Besides, should you be consorting with the enemy?"

He chuckled. "Are you my enemy? I was hoping we could be friends."

"Between this and keeping up with my day job, I don't have time to make friends."

"It's just coffee."

Behind him, he heard Lilly. "I'm in. Let's go." She walked forward and took him by the elbow. As they headed toward the door, Lilly said, "We need a plan to take out all the rest." It was loud enough to make Isabel gasp.

Had she knowingly put a target on his back? It was Lilly, and the answer was, without a doubt, yes.

Chapter 7

Chloe couldn't believe how exhausting an hour-long show could be, but it wasn't really an hour. They started at nine, and it was noon by the time they finished the retakes and set up for the next day. Too bad she didn't have time for a lunch break, but there were cakes to make and croissants to bake.

She took the elevator down to the kitchen to clock in.

"Chloe, glad you're here." Flynn waved her toward his office. "We have a problem."

That was one of the worst things to hear when she came into work. It was right up there with "you're fired" or a letter from the Internal Revenue Service telling you they were doing an audit. The thought left a shiver racing down her spine.

She followed him into his office and took a seat in front of his desk. Any other person might have intimated her. Flynn was her boss for all intents and purposes, but he was also her sister's boyfriend, making him family.

"Don't tell me I have to enter another competition. If you want someone to compete in the food festival, I'm not your girl."

He flopped into his chair and rubbed the scruff on his face. As he dropped his hand, his lips fell into a frown. "How is that going? Today was the first day of the competition. Are you still in the running?" An expression lifted his brows.

Was that hope that she was in, or hope she was out?

"It isn't an automatic elimination." She leaned forward and took a paper and pen from his desk and drew a six-by-six graph. "Six challenges with scores that are added together. Someone leaves after every two." She wrote the names and today's score. "I'm safely in second place today."

His shoulders slumped. "Oh."

"Don't get too excited."

He leaned back, the chair squeaking with the redistribution of his weight. "I was kind of hoping..."

She waited for him to finish his sentence, and because he didn't, it dawned on her. "You were expecting me to fail?"

"No, I know you Mason girls, and there isn't a quitting gene in your body."

"Then what do you want?"

He pressed his lips together until a thin line formed. "It's not what I want but what I need." He pushed a stack of applications her way. "Your number one girl left without notice."

The air whooshed from her lungs. What would she do without Gretchen?

"What do you mean she left?"

He shook his head. "She walked in this morning and said she was moving to California. That's all she told me before she set her uniform on the table and strolled out."

"Oh my God, she just up and left?" Gretchen had been swooning over some guy she met on TikTok. She obsessively watched videos of him dancing and singing and stripping. It was the stripping ones that were on replay all the time. "I can't believe it." Gretchen was the only reason she could compete and maintain her job.

"I hate to lay it all on you, but you'll have to throw the show to get back into the kitchen or find a replacement and get them up to speed. We can't be without a pastry chef for weeks."

"As you said, there isn't a quitting bone in my body." She was in second place and hated that spot. Some people were always stuck. It could be at a certain weight or a particular goal, but her Achilles heel, her position—runner up. And that made her feel so inadequate. "I'll figure it out." She swiped the applications from the table. "If you've got nothing else for me, I'll get started."

"I'll try to send you some help."

She hugged the papers to her chest. "Thanks." With a sigh, she walked out.

Her space in the kitchen was set off from everyone. She pulled down the inventory sheet and the baking chart she'd made for the week. Thankfully, this wasn't a one-person show, and she had part-time bakers. She'd have to call them in because, one thing was for sure, she wasn't quitting the contest. If she gave up now, she'd always wonder if she had it in her to win.

By ten o'clock that night, she was spent but prepped for the next day. All the crew needed to do was bake the bread. After clocking out, she went to her locker but found it empty. Realizing she'd left everything in the conference room, she headed to the "studio" to grab her bag and jacket.

When she got there, she found Isabel on her way out. The poor woman jumped a foot in the air when she turned and saw Chloe approach.

"Oh, Lordy." Her hand came to the cameo pinned on the collar of her shirt. "You scared the bejeezus out of me. What are you doing here?"

Chloe cocked her head. It was a strange question for a woman who was in the same place. She pointed to the table hidden behind a false wall. "I left my bag and jacket."

Isabel hugged her purse to her chest. "It would appear that we're here for the same reason. Sometimes I wonder if my head is attached to my body." She laughed. "Wouldn't that be something? What if you could accessorize with a different head?" She touched her white curls. "I'd pick a younger version."

"I think you're lovely as you are."

Isabel waited for Chloe to get her bag.

"You're a dear." She glanced back at the leaderboard, which was still lit up from earlier today. "And quite a baker. Who would have thought to make capers into brittle?"

Chloe smiled at a memory of her grandfather. On Sundays after family dinner, he'd take her into the kitchen to help make dessert. "Think outside the box," he said on more than one occasion. Fortney Mason was the original Wolfgang Puck.

"My grandfather was a staunch believer in pushing the envelope. Though we never candied capers, we have dipped bacon in caramel and chocolate and rolled it in potato chips. It's out of this world."

Isabel smiled, but the bridge of her nose wrinkled in distaste. She'd seen her try to camouflage her emotions earlier that day, and the same thing happened, and she wondered if that was Isabel's tell. Everyone had a nervous habit that let people know they were less than honest. Maybe that was hers.

"Are you staying at the resort?"

She nodded, sending those pin curls bobbing. "The show put us up."

"Lucky you." That wasn't an option offered her, but she was a late arrival and a local.

They walked out the door and went in separate directions.

Spent by the time she got home but too full of nervous energy to sleep, she made a cup of tea and sat at the island. Within reaching distance was the tattered book with the heart on the cover. She pulled it over and stared.

"What are you about?"

She opened the first page and found a note from its author.

Dear Baker,

Everything I learned about love, I learned from baking.

Everything you need to know about love, you'll learn here.

Because you're reading this, it means you've accepted the challenge of choosing one recipe, perfecting it, and passing on the book.

As with everything in life, baking takes effort. Like love, it can't be rushed.

Have you ever wondered why baked goods require certain ingredients?

We add sugar to bring out our inner sweetness.

Salt gives life its flavor.

Flour is a binder like honesty and faithfulness.

Butter is the guilty pleasure in the mix.

Baking soda lifts like a bright smile on a dull day.

Without these, a cake is not a cake, and a pie is not a pie. Without love, a life isn't worth living.

Baking, like love, should be done with passion.

I challenge you to pick one recipe and only one because love shouldn't be hoarded but shared.

Choose the right recipe, and if you can't decide, open the book to a page and let the recipe choose you.

Share the dessert but not the book. There will be time for that later.

Remember, a perfect cake, or pie, or cookie is like perfect love. It's takes practice, patience, give and take, resourcefulness, perseverance, and often teamwork.

With love,

Adelaide Phelps

She stared at the last line about practice and patience and teamwork. This wasn't advice about love; it was a map for life. Adelaide Phelps was a female Dalai Lama. As for love, Chloe wasn't interested. Who had time for it when there were hundreds of baked goods to make and shows to win?

Though she was tempted to close the book and push it aside, she often tested fate. With her eyes closed, she did what the book said. She let it choose for her. Flipping blindly through the pages, she waited for her internal voice to yell "stop" when it slipped from her hand and fell open to a recipe called Kiss Me Cupcakes.

She glanced at it briefly but didn't have time to bother with a cupcake recipe when she had to be up in six hours.

"Mrs. Phelps, I'll have to bid you good night." She closed the book and pushed it away before gulping her herbal tea and heading to bed.

As she drifted off to sleep, she thought about the recipe name: Kiss Me Cupcakes. If a recipe book could bring love, would she want it? As her lids grew heavy, she was stuck on an unequivocal no. Men were a pain in the ass. As soon as the word ass flashed through her mind, she thought of Mr. Hot Cross Buns, and her last thought was a question. What kind of kisser would Gage Sweet be?

Chapter 8

"Welcome to another episode of *The Great Bake Off*," Ryan Cross said as the cameras recorded. "Competing on this show is no cakewalk, as you can see from yesterday's results." He pointed to the leaderboard, which showed the order the contestants came in the first round. Then the cameras zoomed in for closeups of Lilly's and Isabel's expressions.

Lilly's smile was tight and forced, and Isabel didn't seem bothered in the least. She had that Mrs. Claus quality that made everyone feel at ease.

Gage wondered what Christmas or Easter was like at her house. He imagined homemade gingerbread houses and challah bread baked with colored eggs.

He glanced to his right and took in Chloe, who smiled at the camera. The joy she tried to portray in her smile never got to her eyes, or maybe the dark circles sitting like faint bruises camouflaged whatever happiness she felt sitting in second place.

He inched over and whispered under his breath. "Late night?"

Her fake smile fell, and she gave him what his mother would call the stink eye.

"Rude much?"

"Today's challenge is all about cakes, but not just any cake," Ryan said, interrupting the exchange he had with Chloe. "This cake has to be chocolate with a twist. Our guest judge today is Maximum Cinema's CEO. As a salute to the movies, you must incorporate something you'd find in a movie theater concession stand. Good luck, bakers. You have two hours to complete your project. Time starts now."

Just like yesterday, all the contestants ran toward the supply table—everyone but Chloe. She rubbed her chin and started in on the cake batter. Each station had its own set of ingredients like flour, baking soda, salt. The only community ingredients sat on the table. Gage swiped up the malted milk balls. He decided he'd make a malted milk chocolate cake with a chocolate caramel Milk Dud filling.

He set his ingredients on his prep table and gathered everything else he'd need. This was the challenge he looked forward to. His entire life as a baker, he wanted to bake cakes and cupcakes and cookies, but his father would have none of it. Now was his chance to prove he had what it took to make amazing cakes.

As he measured out his ingredients, Lilly, Matt, and Dwayne ran around their kitchen like chickens without heads. Chloe and Isabel acted as if there wasn't a worry in the world. He understood Chloe's pace. Even if she came in last place today, she wasn't likely to go home. Isabel, on the other hand, should be worried. Anything under third place put her at risk.

"What are you making?" Gage asked Chloe.

On her work surface, she had Raisinets and Goobers, which she dumped into her cake batter. She also had Milk Duds.

"I'm not sure, but we'll see what happens." She opened the box of chocolate-covered caramel candies, cut them into pieces, then put those in the batter before pouring it into cake pans and putting it in the preheated oven.

He carefully measured his baking soda, flour, and cocoa, then mixed them with the wet ingredients. As the mixer did its job, he headed to the stove. It was the only place they had to share. But with six burners, there was plenty to go around.

He dumped his Milk Duds in a pan and added heavy cream so it could melt into what he'd use between layers. Rather than make a two-layer cake, he decided on three, with the center layer being the one with the malted milk balls.

A crash and an expletive came from his left as Matt looked at the cake batter and pans on the floor.

"Dammit," he yelled while stomping his feet. "I don't have time to start over." After another mini tantrum, he went back to mixing.

The host talked about the scores, and if Matt couldn't pull something delicious out of a hat, he'd be out.

Lilly rushed around so quickly she was a blur of orange.

Dwayne stood by his prep table, hands crossed over his chest, looking at the ingredients he had out for the frosting.

"Do I go big?" he asked out loud.

The host loved this kind of interaction. "If you don't, you could go home."

Dwayne smiled. "Theater buttercream frosting with a popcorn garnish coming up." He tossed cubes of butter and powdered sugar into the mixer and turned it on.

Gage did the same, and ten minutes later, like alarm clocks set at five-minute intervals, the oven times blared.

Chloe was the first to pull out her cake, which looked fluffy and perfect. Next was Isabel, whose cake was also perfect. Baking at high altitude was tricky, and he hoped the contestants coming from sea level knew that additional flour and water were required.

Matt shoved new batter into the oven and rushed to make his frosting.

Lilly's cake came out, and she let out a growl that could scare a watchdog. "High altitude," she grumbled.

A Dollop of Delight

He peeked at her cake to see the centers had fallen slightly.

His timer went off, and he popped open the oven expecting to see fluffy, rich chocolate but found three cake pans that had cooked but never risen.

"What the?"

The host and a camera crew rushed over to catch the disaster. One thing Gage knew was never to let them see you sweat. If something went wrong, he needed to pretend it was planned.

"Perfect." He pulled the pans from the oven and brought them to his prep table. The cake looked more brownie than cake, and his mind raced to figure out what went wrong.

"Falling flat, Gage?" Ryan asked.

He shook his head. "Not at all. I knew everyone would bake a traditional cake. This is dense, rich, chocolate cake that's almost like lava cake only better." He hoped he wasn't lying. The flavor should still be present, but the texture could be off.

As the pans cooled, he analyzed his ingredients and went over his recipe. The only thing that could have caused this issue was if he forgot the baking soda, but that was impossible. He specifically remembered measuring it out.

He looked at his competitors, and an awful twist of his gut stopped him short. Surely someone hadn't sabotaged him. There was no way one of these bakers would do that. While he didn't know everyone, they all seemed above cheating.

On a hunch, he opened the baking soda and scooped out a pinch on the end of a spoon. As soon as it hit his tongue, he knew why his cake was better suited as a hockey puck than a winning recipe.

Not wanting to draw attention to the issue on film and have to have them cut the scene out, he continued to create his masterpiece, despite the anger building inside him. This was a competition, but it should've been a fair competition, and by the looks of it, he was the only one who had a flat cake. While Lilly's deflated in the center, that was a measurement issue. Someone targeted him specifically.

At the stove, he stirred his caramel sauce.

"Problem with the cake, honey?" Isabel stood beside him, stirring what looked to be peanut brittle. "You may have fooled the host, but I know a cake that's missing baking soda."

"Not missing," he whispered under his breath. "Someone switched mine out with cornstarch."

Isabel gasped. "No. That's going to create a pasty consistency."

"You're right, but hopefully, it doesn't ruin the taste."

She looked at him with grandmotherly concern. "You know," she leaned in and whispered. "I came back here last night to get my bag and saw Chloe coming out. She said it was to pick up her jacket and bag, but honestly, she has access to everything whenever she wants. She works here."

When he considered his saboteur, Chloe didn't come to mind. His thoughts went immediately to Lilly since she was in last place and had such a strong A-game versus B-game response.

He stirred his caramel sauce. "Do you think it would be her?"

Isabel smiled. "It makes sense, honey. I heard she wasn't the original contestant. That girl fell and broke her leg, so the show pulled the pastry chef from the resort as a fill-in."

He knew she worked at Luxe, and it made sense that she'd feel under the gun to succeed, but by ruining another's chance?

"She had the means and opportunity." Isabel left him with so many questions. She took her brittle to her table, and he returned to his with the caramel sauce.

"Fifteen minutes," Ryan shouted. "Who will be left standing?" He turned to the camera, which panned to all the contestants. "Whose dessert will the judges find Oscar-worthy and whose will fall flat?" He knew they focused the camera on his cake, but what could he do?

He carefully removed the layers from the pans. They were

heavy, which wouldn't bode well for the end result, but when life gave him lemons, he made martinis. He plated the first layer and dripped the warm caramel on top, then put the malted milk ball layer and then the final one. Three layers were originally a bonus but turned into a necessity. He was grateful he had all three. Otherwise, his cake would have come up short in so many ways.

"How's it going?" Chloe asked.

Anger turned and toiled in his gut. "Exactly as you planned."

He wasn't staring at her directly, but he caught the cock of her head and turned to see her confused expression. If she was the saboteur, she was good at playing innocent. No matter who won and who lost today, it would be Chloe going home when he told the director she cheated.

As the clock ticked down and time evaporated, he frosted his cake and dusted the top with malt.

"Time's up. Step away from the cakes."

They cut to commercial, which gave everyone a chance to get water and take a break.

"What did you mean?" Chloe asked.

"Did you have to cheat to win?"

Her hand went to her heart as if he'd wounded her. "What are you talking about?"

"Oh, don't play innocent with me."

"And we're back."

Gage stepped away from Chloe and took his place in front of his cake.

Even though Matt pulled together another batch, he delivered a cake the judges called basic and boring.

Next up was Dwayne, who didn't wow the judges with the buttery cake he'd whipped up. One said it had the texture of regurgitated corn. Isabel wowed the judges with her Nestlé Crunch cake. When they got to Lilly, they were less than impressed. As the judges tasted Chloe's, he simmered. While they loved her frosting, they thought her cake was a little dry. That critique satisfied him. Maybe cheating was the only way for her to win. If so, his question was, why was he her first target?

He needed this win. Sweet Eats wouldn't survive without it. Though he would live without the bakery that had been in his family for over five decades, he wasn't sure his mother could. It was all she knew.

"Last but not least is Gage Sweet. Tell us about your cake."

He smiled. "I think I'll call it Triple Caramel Treachery." As soon as he said the last word, he looked at Chloe. "What I've made for you today is a three-layer dark chocolate cake with caramel drizzle and a dark chocolate malted milk ball frosting."

He held his breath while the judges tasted his disaster. The fact that all three struggled to get the cake off the roofs of their mouths said it was too dense, too gooey, and overly gluey. He was definitely getting the boot. He only hoped to bring the crime to light and get justice.

After deliberating, the three judges gave their critique, which wasn't as unpleasant as he thought. They weren't happy with the texture, but the flavor was there, and they appreciated how he used the challenge ingredients.

As the contestants cleaned their workstations, the show went to commercial, and the judges decided on the fate of one baker.

Ryan directed them to stand side by side. It reminded Gage of one of those war movies where they lined up prisoners for the firing squad. Only this time, the bullet was aimed at him, and it was dipped in betrayal and deceit.

"The judges have chosen this episode's winner. In the number one spot with her Nestlé Crunch cake is Isabel."

The older woman smiled and did a little dance. It was so fun to watch her excitement at the win, especially since she'd placed so low yesterday. All Gage could think of was the win couldn't have gone to a nicer person. Even though Lilly's cake had sunk in the center, she'd risen from the bottom to the second-place position. Chloe came in third, which felt like scrubbing his eyes with sand and diving into the saltwater with them open.

Next, to his surprise, was him. He turned toward Chloe and laughed. "Your plan failed. I'm not going home today." His combined scores kept him safe in the middle. It wasn't where he wanted to be, but considering what he'd just accomplished, he was proud of the fourth-place finish. Matt followed him. When the scores from the last competition were added to today's, Matt ended up on the bottom.

"Matt, I'm sorry, but you're out." The spotlight highlighting his station turned off, and they were down to five. He was still in the running. As soon as the cameras were no longer filming, he walked over to the director and pulled him aside.

He explained what happened and who he thought was responsible.

Five minutes later, after the director, the set designer, and the host conferred, they called Chloe and him to the side.

She stared at him like she had no clue what was going on. The woman didn't have an ounce of fear or regret showing anywhere. If he were about to get accused of cheating, he would've been sweating like a sinner in church. But Chloe's face only showed confusion.

"It has come to our attention that you may be responsible for switching ingredients to tilt the scales in your favor."

"I what?" Chloe asked.

The show was being too kind with their words, so he came out and said what they didn't. "You cheated and tried to sabotage me to get me eliminated."

She cocked her head to the other side, causing her neck to pop. "I what?"

Her response was surprising, considering she was guilty.

There was usually some kind of tell when someone lied, but her shock appeared genuine.

"You switched the baking soda for cornstarch."

She hopped back like he'd set her on fire. "I did not. I would never cheat."

He'd heard the rumors surrounding her family at the Aspen Food Festival and how her father wanted her older sister to steal an ingredient from his competitor's table so he would win.

"Seems to be a family trait. If you can't do it on your own, then make sure your competition can't either. That's how it works, right? One year it's foie gras, and another it's a leavening agent."

"Wait. I did nothing of the sort. I'd never cheat. If I can't win fair and square, then I don't want the win."

The hard stomping of heels against the tile floor drew all their attention.

Chloe appeared to stagger back. "You called my boss?"

Chapter 9

The last time Chloe was this scared was when she'd cut school to avoid the tenth-grade history exam. Her classmates had come up with some master plan to cheat on the test, and she didn't want to be implicated by association, so she left the school campus and went straight to La Grande Mason.

When she walked inside, the look on her father's face made her wonder if cheating would've been better. The look on Allie's face made her feel the same, but for very different reasons. Allie thought she cheated, and it disappointed her father that she hadn't taken the chance to get a leg up in the class, considering her grade was barely a C.

"What the hell is going on here?" Allie walked to the group and fisted her hips.

Chloe was generally quiet and compliant, but not today. If she didn't stand up for herself, who would?

"They are accusing me of sabotaging the competition."

Like a good parent, Allie turned to the producer. "Those are mighty big allegations that jeopardize not only the reputation of Chloe but also Luxe Resorts. Do you have proof?"

Chloe hadn't considered what it meant for Luxe Resorts, but it would be bad for the resort's reputation if they sponsored a baking contest and cheated to win.

Leo shook his head. "We have an accusation and an eyewitness but no physical proof."

"An eyewitness?" Confusion washed over her like a flash flood, causing her stomach to flip and turn. "Someone saw me do something?"

Gage shifted between his feet. "Isabel said she saw you coming out of this room last night."

Chloe's mind reeled. She couldn't deny that she'd been in the room, but it was to get her jacket and bag. Something didn't sit right with her. Nothing sat right when she was in the hot seat for something she didn't do, but it was the accusation.

"That's not true."

Leo quirked his brow. "You weren't in here last night?"

A ribbon of fear spiraled up and then tightened around her spine, making her lose the sensation in her legs. She was certain she'd collapse. As if feeling her distress, Gage gripped her elbow. Her accuser was also her savior. How funny was that?

Once the white spots and dizziness subsided, she shook free from his grasp.

"I was here, but that's not how things went down. Isabel said that I was coming out while she walked in?"

Everyone looked at Gage. "That's what she said."

A misunderstanding was fixable. "That's not true. It was Isabel who was coming out when I walked inside. She said she forgot her bag, which was why I was in here. I finished my shift and remembered that I'd placed my bag under the table behind that false wall." She pointed to where her belongings were on that day as well.

"You admit to being here?"

All eyes were on her.

"Yes, I was here, but keep in mind that Isabel was too."

Gage frowned. "You're going to blame that sweet old lady?"

She stomped her foot. "Don't forget that sweet old lady just blamed me. That doesn't make her all that sweet in my book. Also, don't forget that I was the fill-in, so while I'd love to win this competition, I didn't apply to compete." She turned toward Allie. "You forced me to do it. Keep that in mind when you're accusing me. Sure, now that I'm here, I'm in it to win it. I've got something to prove, but I'd never accept a win if I got it from cheating. I'm appalled that any of you would consider that to be true." She sucked in a breath, hoping it would give her strength. "Also, ask yourself why I'd sabotage Gage? If I were you, I'd be looking at the two people who had the most to lose after yesterday's competition. That was Lilly and Isabel. I was safely in second and not at risk of going home today."

"How do we solve this dilemma?"

Allie smiled. "We'll get our head of security to pull the tapes." She turned to Chloe. "Do you have coverage in the bakery?"

Chloe had a crew on today, but it was the night shift where she was short. "I do until tonight."

Allie frowned. "I'll get Flynn to cover your shift. It would be better if you stayed home until this got resolved."

How was it that one accusation sidelined her entire life? "I'm guilty until proven innocent?"

Allie sighed. "It's not like that. I just want to protect everyone in the process, and until I can get the tapes, it's best if everyone takes a break."

Luckily there were two days between today's taping of the show and the next competition. But would it matter? They'd already painted her as the criminal and Gage the victim.

"You know what's interesting to me?" She didn't wait for anyone to answer. "My accuser isn't even here, and she should also be a suspect." She turned toward Gage. "I agree, someone switched your ingredients, but it wasn't me." She couldn't be sure it was Isabel. Looking at the sweet older woman, she wouldn't have guessed she'd have it in her to cheat, either. Isabel reminded Chloe of her Grandma Mason, and she didn't have a deceitful bone in her body.

She marched over and grabbed her jacket and bag. "I'll be at home if you need me."

She opened the door, and Gage rushed out behind her. "I'm sorry."

"Yeah, so am I." She kept moving forward. "I can't believe I wondered what kissing you would be like."

He caught up with her. "You wanted to kiss me?"

"Funny, huh?" She moved toward the elevator that would take her to the garage. "Imagine that. Last night I thought about how your lips would taste, and today, all I want to do is punch you in the mouth." The elevator door opened, and she stepped inside. "I'm not your enemy, Gage, but someone is, and you better figure it out quickly, or you'll be gone from the competition." The door started to close, but she put her foot out to stop it. "Maybe you sabotaged yourself and accused me to get me removed. I would've thought you'd want to win on merit alone. I'll have to give it to you; it's a clever way to cut down the competition." As the doors closed, she watched everything about the proud-looking man cave in.

Everything between the resort and her apartment was a blur. As she entered her space, she tossed her keys on the table by the door and went straight to the kitchen. Times like this required sustenance in the form of flour, sugar, and lots of fat. Although she baked that afternoon, she pulled out the ingredients to make something from her cupboard. If her grandmother was still alive, she knew she'd be right there to hug her and help her create something sweet for her life, but Grandma Mason was gone, and no one could fill her shoes. Glancing at the cookbook on the counter, she smiled.

"Adelaide Phelps, I need some love, so you're up." She opened the book to the recipe that fate had chosen for her. Kiss Me Cupcakes. Right now, she would rename them Kiss My Ass Cupcakes.

She poured herself a glass of wine because even though it was just after lunchtime, it was five o'clock somewhere. And who made that silly rule, anyway? Why did people have to eat eggs and bacon or cereal for breakfast, sandwiches, soups, and salads for lunch, and something heavy like steak and potatoes for dinner? Why was ice cream or cupcakes a dessert and not the main course? Why in the hell didn't people drink wine in the morning instead of coffee?

"Probably because operating machinery while drunk is illegal. If it weren't, there would be a lot of day drinkers." How funny that she could hold complete conversations by herself, but what choice did she have? There was no one to cry to. Her mother and father were inaccessible, and her sister was building a life that Chloe didn't want to color with her problems.

She stared at the book and the handwritten note from Adelaide. The woman had excellent penmanship.

Dear Baker,

You might ask why I named these delicious treats Kiss Me Cupcakes. I'll tell you why. I first made these cupcakes when I was a young girl. This was before my Sam started courting me. I used to sit in the church pew two rows behind him and swoon. I only saw the back of his head and wished I could see his face and those lips that I wanted to kiss.

Back then, I had no idea what a kiss felt like, but all the girls I knew couldn't stop talking about the boys and rating their kisses. Sam's name never came up, thankfully. I had loved that boy all my life, and I wanted him to save his kisses for me.

But that doesn't explain the cupcakes. My momma once told me the way to a man's heart was through his stomach. My specialty was sweets, so I figured if I could get the perfect mixture of butter, flour, and eggs in his mouth, then I had a chance of winning his heart.

That's how we get to the perfect part. What I learned from making cupcakes is that nothing is ever perfect for everyone. I practiced and practiced until I was sure I'd made the perfect cupcake, but when I gave one to my daddy, he wasn't much impressed. I gave him a plain white cupcake, and he taught me a valuable lesson.

It's not the cupcake that truly matters but what you put into it. When you make a cupcake, you're making a cake for one person and should design it with that person in mind. That's why this recipe is "perfect." You can take something basic and turn it into something amazing. It's kind of like taking a friendship and turning it into the grand love of your life.

I decided that if the way to a man's heart was through his stomach, then I needed to know what my Sam liked to put in his mouth. That started our friendship. We began with bits of conversation after church. I'd see a kid eating raisins and ask Sam if he liked them. Or when the orange trees were fruiting, and the citrus fragrance filled the air, I got more information. It turned out that Sam wasn't all that picky.

I already knew that food was like people. High quality was better. That didn't mean that they had to be rich. Wealth came in many forms. A person could be rich in money but poor in other ways. Sam didn't have any monetary wealth to speak of, but he was a millionaire when it came to kindness and compassion, and that was wealth I'd always be able to bank on.

Back to the cupcakes. Sam was a simple man, so I made the same cupcake I made my father, but I added a little surprise—a dollop of delight in the form of some strawberry preserves I tucked in the center. I'd spent my entire summer watching that boy eat, and he always chose the simplest form of food. That told me Sam didn't like a lot of fuss. He just wanted something simple and sweet. When I brought a single frosted cupcake to Sam, it was like I'd *offered him the sun and moon and all the stars in between. He took a bite, and then he kissed me.*

So, the lesson in this recipe (yes, there's always something to learn) is that you can't truly expect perfection if you haven't mastered the basics. People are like cupcakes: some are simple, and some are complex. We are all different flavors. One isn't better than the next. It's just that some flavors are more suited to our palate. There's a Sam out there for everyone. Are you paying attention to the ingredients of the individual? It certainly makes a difference in the end product.

Adelaide Phelps

Chloe made sure she had all the ingredients for the cupcakes. She wasn't looking for a Sam; she was looking for a sugar high.

1 1/3 cups (185 grams/6.5 ounces) all-purpose flour

    1 teaspoon baking powder

    1/4 teaspoon salt

    1/2 cup (1 stick/115 grams) butter, softened (no margarine or lard here.)

    1 cup (200 grams/7 ounces) granulated sugar

    2 large eggs at room temperature (If you have a chicken coop, just grab a few from under that chicken's butt.)

    1 teaspoon vanilla extract (use the good stuff because remember quality counts)

    1/2 cup (120 ml) whole milk

Instructions

Preheat oven to 350F/180C. Line muffin tin with cupcake liners and set aside.

In a medium bowl, sift together flour, baking powder, and salt and set aside.

Beat together butter and sugar until light and fluffy. Then add in the eggs, one at a time, mixing well after each addition. Add in the vanilla extract and beat until combined. Next, add half of the dry ingredients and mix. Add in the milk and beat until absorbed. Add the other half of the dry ingredients and fold until the batter is smooth. Do not over mix—the less you mix, the lighter the cake will be.

Feel free to customize your cupcake by adding chocolate chips or fruit bits or jam. As long as you don't change the liquid to flour ratio, you should be fine. Cupcakes are a lot like people; they can be filled with all kinds of magic. Maybe your cupcake isn't the vanilla version. If that's the case, look a little harder and dig a little deeper for the surprises inside.

Once the batter is ready, divide it evenly between the cups, filling them about 3/4 full. Bake for 15-20 minutes or until a toothpick inserted into the center comes out clean. Allow cupcakes to sit for 10 minutes, then remove from the pan and allow to cool completely on a wire rack. Frost with my favorite buttercream icing.

Ingredients

1 cup (225 g/2 sticks) unsalted butter, softened to room temperature

1/8 teaspoon salt

4 cups (480 g) powdered sugar, sifted, plus more as needed

3 tablespoons heavy cream

2 teaspoons pure vanilla extract

1 teaspoon freshly squeezed lemon juice

Instructions

In the bowl, beat butter and salt until smooth and creamy, then add 2 cups powdered sugar and mix until combined. Add another 2 cups and beat until completely smooth. Add cream, vanilla, and lemon juice and beat until fluffy. Incorporate more sugar as needed until desired consistency.

Like the cupcakes, the frosting can be full of surprises, too, by adding ingredients like fruit jam, lemon curd, orange zest, chocolate, and more.

Chloe sat there and pondered the recipe and its message about people and what they're made of. She was furious with Gage for not confronting her first, but then again, at least he didn't throw the fit Matt had on camera. Instead, Gage addressed the problem in private, which meant he wasn't trying to humiliate her but to get to the bottom of a sticky situation. She didn't know what was in the center of Gage, but she couldn't believe it was something distasteful. Isabel wasn't the type of person she would expect to cheat, but who else was there? And who else would point the finger but the guilty party?

She preheated the oven and mixed the ingredients. For today, she wouldn't add anything. These cupcakes would be a reflection of how she felt inside—empty.

Chapter 10

Gage dreaded facing Chloe today. When the producer asked him to come in, that feeling washed over him. It wasn't that he didn't want to see her. Seeing her was a delight. She was kind of like the pretty sprinkles on a cake—fun and made everything better.

As he walked into Luxe, he passed Isabel, who was chatting with a stagehand. The woman made friends with everyone. Then again, she had that sweet demeanor of everyone's grandma—the kind of woman who would have cookies and milk on the table when you visited and not just any cookie but the homemade kind that were just out of the oven warm.

Then again, how sweet could she be if she was ready to throw Chloe under the bus without proof? And what did that say about him? He'd done the same. Someone had to answer for the damage. He could've been booted from the show if Matt hadn't dropped his cake and had to start over again. Gage would've been sitting far at the bottom and at risk of being sent home.

Wasn't it ironic how he started out being a reluctant player and was now intent on staying? If he was honest with himself, he rather liked the competition. It was exciting to see where he'd stack up against other bakers. Sitting in the middle didn't give him the confidence he needed. His father's voice still rang in his head, talking about how stupid adding sweets to the menu would be when they'd been known as a bread bakery for decades.

Maybe he was right. Adding items that fell into the average range wouldn't help their dwindling business. The only way it would work was if he won the competition, and he couldn't do that if there was someone in the mix working against him.

"Ah, you're here." Leo walked toward him. "I've asked Chloe and Isabel to meet us here too."

The mention of Chloe made his stomach turn into knots. It was one of those gut reactions he'd get when he knew he was wrong about something.

"Okay, did the resort pull the security tapes?"

Leo nodded. "We'll discuss that when everyone is here."

He stood next to Leo and waited. A few minutes later, Isabel walked over, followed by Chloe.

"Should I prepare myself for incarceration?" Chloe held out her arms as if waiting for cuffs.

"Are you guilty?" Isabel asked.

Chloe narrowed her eyes. "You and I both know I'm not."

"Now that we're all here, we'll head to the corporate offices upstairs." He looked right and left. "I'm a little lost. Can you lead the way, Chloe?"

"Yep." She turned right and walked down the hallway to the lobby and a bank of elevators. "The end one is the only one that stops on the thirteenth floor."

"Thirteen?" Isabel asked. "I didn't think hotels used that floor number because of superstition."

"You can skip the number, but if the building is tall enough, then it will always have a thirteenth floor despite the numbering system. I suppose Luxe decided to make it the corporate floor."

She pushed the button, and the elevator arrived. Climbing

inside, she hit the number thirteen, and they were whisked up. When the door opened, Allie was standing by the employee conference room.

"We'll be in here." Her heels clicked on the stone floor.

Everyone shuffled into the conference room where the head of security, a robust man named Paul Bradley, stood in front of a TV monitor.

He waited for everyone to take a seat and then turned on the monitor.

"This is the security footage from the day in question." He fast-forwarded the tape to show at least a dozen people entering and exiting. "Sadly, the false walls the set designer put up hinder the view, and we can't see anything that happens in the kitchens, but you can see here, Isabel enters without her bag as claimed and exits with it. The same for Chloe. As the head of security, there is no way we can say either of you had ill intent. The security footage is inconclusive. And because the integrity of Luxe and *The Great Bake Off* is in question, we will secure the facility after each taping. Also, no bags will be allowed in the building." He looked at Isabel. "You are staying in the hotel and can leave your belongings in your room and pocket your key." He turned to face Chloe. "You have an employee locker."

He turned off the monitor and nodded at Allie before he left.

"Well, that settles it."

Isabel cleared her throat. "I'd like to know why I was even being considered. I'm appalled that anyone would think I'd stoop so low."

Gage was tired of all the mudslinging. "According to the video, you had as much opportunity as Chloe." He turned to Chloe. "I'm sorry I didn't speak to you first."

She shot daggers in his direction. "I have work to do." She glanced at Allie. "I still have a job, right?"

Allie nodded. "Your job was never in question, Chloe. We just needed to investigate the accusation." She turned toward Isabel. "In the future, I'd be careful who I accused, especially if it also implicates you. As Paul said, everyone is a suspect. Lots of people had access to the set and, therefore, the ingredients. What this has taught us is that we need to be diligent. Locking up the site will be our priority."

"I've got a job to do." Chloe pivoted and walked out.

Gage chased after her. "Hey, wait up."

She didn't slow down but rather sped up, and he had to run to catch up with her.

She got to the elevator and tapped her foot on the tile until the door opened, and she rushed inside. Before she could close the doors, he stepped inside with her. As soon as they were between floors, he pushed the emergency stop, making a loud alarm ring. She stared at the floor.

"Hey, I'm sorry. In my gut, I knew it wasn't you, but it was an automatic response. Please look at me." He pleaded. "Can you honestly say you wouldn't have brought it to someone's attention?"

She lifted her head, and the fury in her eyes bore into him. "I would've never thrown you under the bus."

"That wasn't my intention. I didn't rush over and say I thought you were the instigator; I just said that someone had switched my baking powder with cornstarch and that Isabel thought you might be the one who did it because she saw you coming out of the room as she entered."

"Her memory is faulty. It was the other way around, but I said that, and no one listened. Now I'm a suspect, and I lost a day of work, and in my bosses' minds, there's a shadow of doubt about my integrity. You did that." She fisted her hips. "And don't tell me you didn't think it was me. You even accused me of cheating at the Aspen Food Festival. That was low." She reached past him and pushed the emergency button to disengage the alarm, and the elevator dropped with a shudder and began its descent.

"Is the rumor not true?"

She grimaced. "No, it's true, but it wasn't me. That was my sister, and she wouldn't cheat either. That's why we both work here. We've been disowned and kicked out of the family business. You see ... sometimes you have to make the hard decisions."

The door opened to the kitchens on the first floor, and he followed her out. She spun around to face him. "You can't be here unless you're an employee. I could use a baker, but you'd have to apply and work for me. Lord knows you wouldn't want to work for someone so slimy." She marched away from him.

He stood in the wake of her anger but got an idea. He climbed back into the elevator and pushed floor thirteen.

As he exited, he found Allie walking down the hallway.

"Excuse me." He rushed forward.

She stopped and turned. "Gage, right?"

"Yes, I'm sorry to cause so many problems."

She shrugged. "I can't say I wouldn't do the same. A contest should be fair."

"True, but the way things went down wasn't fair to Chloe. She seems like a good person, and how everything happened wasn't okay."

Allie smiled. "You're old enough to know that life isn't fair. As for Chloe, I never thought she was guilty. The Mason girls are honest to a fault. That's my experience, anyway." She looked over her shoulder. "I'm getting a coffee. Would you like one?"

"Sure."

She walked another ten feet and turned into what appeared to be an employee lounge. On the counter was a fancy coffee maker. Standing in front of it was a beautiful brunette.

"Hey, Allie. You want a latte?"

Allie nodded. "Gage, this is Dani, our general manager." She pointed to him. "And this is Gage, one contestant in the bake-off."

Dani handed the first cup to Allie. "You want a latte too? I make the best."

"Sold," he said.

Allie pointed to a small table. "I'm assuming you're stalking me for a reason?" She lifted her brows and took a seat.

"I wouldn't call it stalking, but yes, I came up here to speak to you. You're the HR person, right?"

"Among other things, but yes."

"I hear you need a baker. While I can't be your long-term solution, I'm happy to be a temporary fill-in while you find your perfect match."

She stared at him like he was speaking a foreign language. "Why would you do that?"

Dani handed him a latte and went back to the machine.

"I'm trying to make amends. I put Chloe in a bad situation, and I'd love to help ease some of her burdens. I've run my bakery for some time now, so I'm familiar with the commercial end of things. This could be a boon for Luxe. Even though I'd be a temporary hire, I believe Chloe or I will win, and that win could be attached to Luxe."

"Why do you think it will be you or her?"

What could he say but the truth? "I don't think either one of us has a losing bone in our body."

"You two are more alike than different. That was exactly what she told me when I told her she was competing. She said something like, 'I don't have a losing bone in my body. I can't lose, or it will destroy me.'"

"That seems dramatic."

Allie laughed. "That's exactly what I said, but we haven't lived in her shoes, and I think being a Mason isn't all it's cracked up to be. Imagine having a world-renowned grandfather, a famous father, and you work at Luxe." She rolled her eyes. "I'm not saying

Luxe isn't a great place to work because it is, but people like Chloe and Gabby don't work for others. Others work for them."

"That's why I'm here. I've closed my bakery while I'm competing, but truth be told, I could use the income. My cat Sassy likes to eat. You can use the help, and I've got to make amends with Chloe."

Dani finished making her latte and moved toward the door. "Don't forget the part where you confess to being sweet on Chloe."

He wasn't the blushing type, but the heat of one stung his cheeks. He'd be lying if he said he wasn't attracted to her. She was cute, spirited, and talented, which was a combination that worked for him.

"You like her?"

He considered his answer. "She's all right."

Dani chuckled. "What are you, five? Just admit it. It might get you the job. You know, honesty being the best policy and all."

"Fine," he said with an exasperated breath. "I like her, but I don't know her that well and given the situation that happened, I'm not likely to get close enough to her to get to know her, but if I'm working with her, then that allows her to know me as well. I'm not a bad guy. I try to do good things. That whole situation got away from me."

Allie giggled. "I've never played cupid."

Dani cocked her head. "Sure, you have." She opened her eyes in that don't-you-remember way. It was like the girls had a secret code, and I wasn't allowed to have the cipher.

"I don't need a cupid. I just need an opportunity to prove I'm not a bad guy."

"Yep." Allie grinned. "He likes her." She sipped from her coffee. "Tell you what. If you can convince her to hire you, I'll give you a temporary job. I've put that poor girl in a bind, and I owe her some help, but if you so much as do one thing to annoy her, you're out of here."

"My presence will annoy her, but I promise to help her."

Dani laughed. "This should be fun."

Gage thought about Chloe's expression when he showed up to work. "Oh yay, it's going to be a laugh a minute." He downed his latte and rose to put his cup in the trash. "Can I start now?"

"Sure." Allie stood. "I'll walk you down. I wouldn't miss this moment for anything."

They made it to the elevator and down to the first-floor kitchens. He followed Allie around a corner to where Chloe was bending over a mixer. Her backside was facing him, and he had to say it was a pleasant view.

"Chloe?" Allie said.

Chloe startled and spun around to see them.

"What's he doing here?"

"He's a new temporary hire to help you until you find a replacement for your last assistant."

Seeing a rack with clean aprons, Gage grabbed one. "Where would you like me to start?"

Chapter 11

"What the hell is going on here?" Chloe looked at Allie, who had a slight smile on her face.

"I've always been told to keep your friends close and your enemies closer." Allie nodded toward Gage, who tied the apron around his waist. "Mr. Sweet has generously offered to help out while we're shorthanded."

"That's like letting the fox in the henhouse." She couldn't believe what was happening.

Allie shrugged. "We needed help, and he needed a job."

Chloe narrowed her eyes. "He's got a bakery."

Gage moved forward. "He's right here, and while he does have a bakery, it's closed until further notice."

"You kids play nice. I expect to see great things coming out of here. Who would've thought we'd have two contestants vying for the win?" Allie bounced on her heels like an excited child. She looked at Gage. "I'll send down your paperwork later." With that, she turned and walked away.

"What are you doing?" Chloe disengaged the locking mechanism from the large floor mixer and hefted the bowl onto the table.

She didn't need the gym. Working in a bakery was like lifting weights on the daily.

"I'm making amends."

She walked past him to the rack that held muffin pans. Muddled emotions plagued her. She didn't know how to feel about anything.

"I don't need your help, and I don't think it's my responsibility to make you feel better for the mistake you made."

"You're right." He pulled the pans from her hand and lined them up on the table. He reached past her for the cooking spray and lightly coated the pans before washing his hands at the nearby sink and donning a pair of gloves. He moved around her like he'd worked there all his life. Then again, he had worked in a bakery.

"I don't know why you insist on making my life hard. I've done nothing to you."

"You're right," he repeated. He picked up a scoop, filling the muffin tins. "Do you add anything to your corn muffins?" He shifted around her to get to the trays farthest from him. "When we make them at the bakery, sometimes we sprinkle cheese or add in jalapeno."

She shook her head to get him out of it. He'd been there since that day she met him. There was something about Gage Sweet that pushed her to extremes. One day she was thinking about what his lips were like, and the next, she considered bodily harm.

"I'll get the cheese." She moved toward the bakery's refrigeration unit and pulled out the cheddar.

As he filled pans, she sprinkled cheese. What would've taken her an hour to do took about twenty minutes. Having him there was not pleasant, but it was helpful. He was like a splinter that rubbed her the wrong way. She needed to find a way to remove him from her life, but maybe she'd wait until the prep was done for the day.

"What's next?" He lifted the large mixing bowl from the table and took it to the sink.

"Croissants."

"That's my specialty. How many do you need?"

"We have three baking shifts, but for our shift ... let's make three hundred." What was she doing? The man was here for half an hour max, and she was thinking of him as part of her team already.

"Our shift. I like that."

She let out a deep throat sound that was half grunt and half growl. "Don't get used to it. I'm only letting you stay because Allie put you here. If it were up to me, all I'd see is your backend walking to the elevator."

He smiled, and the room somehow seemed brighter. "I've never had complaints about my back end."

"I wouldn't know as I've never checked you out."

He spun around to show her the goods, and she had to admit, he looked mighty fine in those jeans.

"What do you think?" He turned to face her.

"I think you need a pair of black pants to be in uniform."

"You're no fun." He went back to the bowl and rinsed it out before drying and putting it on the stand.

"I'm lots of fun, but you'll never find out." This was awkward banter because she found him attractive, but she didn't want to forget so quickly that he'd been the one to throw her under the bus.

That didn't seem quite right. Isabel threw her under the bus, but Gage didn't put the brakes on before running over her, then backing up and doing it again.

"Says the girl who thinks about my lips."

He had a point. "That was before."

"We'll see."

A Dollop of Delight

She pointed toward the dry storage. "This isn't the dating game. It's work, and you should probably get to it before I fire you."

"That would be the biggest mistake of your life."

Nope, liking you was.

She walked away and picked up the list left by the last shift. She had blueberry and raspberry muffins to make and a couple of cakes. *The Great Bake Off* wasn't all that hard. Cakes were cakes, muffins were muffins, and cupcakes were cupcakes. What made it challenging was the surprise ingredients. Hopefully, she wouldn't run into crazy stuff like durian, or caviar, or kimchi. She pulled off salmon and capers, but she didn't know what she'd do if she got fermented cabbage or fish eggs.

For the next two hours, they worked in silence. Gage prepared several hundred perfect croissants and let them sit to rise. She finished the muffins before they moved on to the cakes. Once they finished the cakes, she looked at the list again.

"We're finished."

He looked over her shoulder at the list. "It says quick-breads."

"No, it's okay; I don't want to do those right now."

He took the clipboard. "We can whip these up in no time. Let's start the next shift off right."

"No, it's okay."

He assembled the dry ingredients as if he knew a recipe by heart.

"Just stop," she said with a little too much force. "I just ... I just." She covered her face with her hand. There was no way she'd show weakness in front of him.

He stopped and stared at her. "You want to talk about it?"

"No, I don't."

"Then let's not talk, but we are making the bread. How shitty would it be for the boss lady not to fulfill her end of the bargain?"

He was right. Normally she scheduled quick breads on other shifts. She didn't know why, but she could never get them right.

She messed with the recipe and paid attention to the high-altitude instructions. She tried under-mixing and over-mixing and mixing normally, but they always turned out wrong.

"What kind are we making?"

Maybe this was the time to put her ego away and learn something.

"Do you have a specialty?"

"We don't make any sweets in the bakery to speak of."

It was a crying shame because that seemed a no-brainer. "You're truly missing an opportunity for some pretty sweet branding."

He groaned. "I told my dad that for years, but he was old school, and you didn't mess with success."

"Is the bakery successful?"

She watched the light dim in his eyes. "No. In truth, if I don't win this competition, I'll have to close it. My mom is much like my father and has dug her heels deep to keep it the way it was fifty years ago."

"You can't grow if you don't change."

"Exactly." He rummaged around the ingredients and came back with bananas, walnuts, cranberries, and oranges. "My sister entered me into this competition. I didn't want to do it. I've spent a lifetime disappointing my family. I could hear my dad from beyond telling me I'd never win."

She moved in next to him and looked at the ingredients he'd pulled out, mentally taking inventory.

"I got shanghaied into it when a contestant broke her leg and couldn't participate."

He smiled. "I thought it was odd that they'd pick several contestants from the area. While Lilly has shops everywhere, the one here is her home base."

She wasn't sure if she had a right to nose around, but she was curious. "Are you and Lilly a thing?"

He was quick to shake his head. "No, I mean, we dated once, but there wasn't much chemistry. You know, it's either there, or it isn't, and it wasn't. Not like you and I."

She laughed. "Oh, that's not chemistry unless we're talking fire and gasoline."

"Call it what you want, but there's something. I wouldn't be here if there wasn't. I feel bad about what happened."

She gnawed on the inside of her cheek. "I considered what you did, and I get it. Now that you told me about the bakery, I get it more. A lot is riding on this for you."

"There is." He measured out flour, baking soda, and salt and put them into a bowl. "I told my mom that if I won, we were changing things up. The bakery would reopen but under my terms." He turned and smiled. "I've always wanted to make cupcakes." He leaned in and whispered, "I'm a closet cupcake maker. Don't tell anyone."

She loved the way he joked and teased, even though she hadn't been all that warm and kind to him.

"If we're telling secrets ..." She wasn't sure why she was going to tell him, but they had to build trust somewhere, so why not start here. "I can't make bread to save my life."

His mouth opened into a delicious O, accentuating his perfect lips. Her thoughts went back to how they'd feel against hers.

"Let's remedy that. It all starts with the basic batter, and at high altitude, things dry out too fast, so I add a little more moisture through extra wet ingredients like egg or banana."

He showed her his basic batter recipe, and she mentally made a note of it.

"Next, you can add anything you want. It's only limited by your imagination. What you put inside is the surprise."

"There's a baker named Adelaide Phelps that might agree with you. She says it's what's on the inside that truly matters."

He shrugged. "Sure, but things can be good in their purest

form, too. Not everyone likes a fuss. Sometimes it's the simple things that trip your trigger."

She wanted to laugh at his description. "Well, my trigger doesn't get tripped all that often."

"That's too bad. A little trigger tripping can go a long way." He pulled his lower lip between his teeth in that I'm-too-sexy-for-my-apron kind of way.

Why did her mind keep going there with him?

Because no one has tripped my trigger in a long time.

She wanted to hate him, but it was so hard when he was so nice.

"Since we're making the banana nut, I picked the ripest bananas because they're the sweetest." He pointed to the dry ingredients. "I also add cinnamon."

He showed her from start to finish, and as he poured the batter into pans, he said, "The key to not getting a heavy loaf is in the folding of the ingredients. You want it to incorporate everything but with a light hand."

In her mind, adding more moist ingredients meant a heavier bread, but she'd see how his bread turned out before deciding.

After that batch went into the oven, he told her to make the next batch, and he'd guide her on the ingredients.

When it came time to mix in the cranberries and orange zest, he stood behind her, took her hand in his, and showed her how to fold the ingredients softly. "Making quick bread is like making love."

His voice whispered in her ear and weakened her knees.

"How's that?" she asked breathily. It took everything in her not to let her head fall back to his shoulder.

"Don't rush it. You need to take your time." He moved the spoon in a slow, languid caress across the batter. "Just when you think it's finished, you go that extra bit to pull it to perfection."

She swore his lips touched her cheek, but as soon as it registered, he stepped away, leaving her flushed and hot.

"Let's get these into the oven." He lined up several pans and poured the batter into them.

She slid them into the preheated oven and set the timer. If she was flushed when she backed away, at least she could blame the heat.

"You want a coffee?" she asked.

"Dying for one."

They made their way into the restaurant, where her friend leaned against the counter of the server station.

"What are you doing here?" she asked Kinsley.

"It's boys' night out, and Julian took Matthew to a movie. Some superhero flick, so when Flynn called and asked if I could cover, I was happy to."

She turned to Gage. "This is Gage Sweet. He's..." She wasn't sure how to describe him. Was he her competitor? Her employee? "He's—"

"I'm a friend."

She liked the sound of that. How long had it been since she had one?

Kinsley smiled. "Are you one of the contestants?"

"I am," Gage said. "And a temporary employee."

"And handsome." Kinsley smiled. "Funny how things work out." She grabbed a tray and moved forward. "You kids have fun."

Chloe poured two coffees. "What now?" She had no idea what she was truly asking, but there were a lot of questions like if the quick bread would turn out. What would it be like on the set the next day? And that same old question about his lips. She caught herself staring at them for far too long, and when she looked up, he was right in front of her.

"You don't have to wonder. Just taste." He moved in and pressed his lips to hers.

Oh, holy hotness.

Chapter 12

There are kisses that you remember, and then there are those you'll never forget. Kissing Chloe would be burned into his memory for a lifetime. Sweet lips. Soft moan. Tasted like spun sugar. She was irresistible.

She stared at his lips like she was starving for them. He never left a girl hungry or wanting, so he fed her. That kiss lasted until her friend Kinsley came back and brushed past them to get the coffee pot. They separated like they'd been sprayed with a hose.

"We should check the quick bread." Chloe picked up her coffee mug and dashed out of the server station.

"Be good to her, or you'll deal with me."

Gage laughed. "You don't need to threaten me. Being good to her is my goal." He left, not knowing exactly what happened, but he didn't feel alone for the first time in a long time.

What kind of reception would he get today when he showed up at the set?

Last night he followed Chloe back to the kitchen, but she said very little. And when the quick breads came out of the oven perfectly baked, she did a little jump for joy. He hoped the kiss would do the same for her, but she pretended it didn't happen, and he never mentioned it either.

He moved through the doors and found the set director racing around like her hair was on fire.

She rolled in what looked like a tall locker and opened it with a key. "Gather 'round, my people." She made a come here motion with her arms and waited for the five remaining bakers to follow her bidding. Chloe stood on the opposite side of him. Her eyes drifted to the locker and found their way back to him. She pretended not to be affected by the kiss, but the way she stared at his lips made him believe she wanted it to happen again.

When he caught her gawking a second time, her cheeks turned a crimson red.

"Because of recent allegations, I am locking up supplies at the end of the show, and they won't be unlocked until right before the next episode. We will rotate all products, so what you used today might not be what you get tomorrow. This is to avoid any other accusations of cheating."

Hildy stared at him.

"Hey, I'm not the perpetrator but the victim."

Chloe let out a growl. "I'm also a victim because someone falsely accused me." She glared at Isabel.

"Don't look at me. I just reported what I saw."

"You need an eye exam." Chloe fisted her hips. "You and I both know, and so does the crew, that you arrived first, and I came in second. Get your story straight."

Isabel stumbled back like she was about to fall. Dwayne and Lilly rushed to her side, and after several moments of babying and cajoling, the show was about to start.

Ryan, the host, told everyone to take their places, and all the bakers stood in the center of the kitchen facing the camera.

Gage was next to Chloe, and he leaned in. "How'd you sleep?"

She smiled and talked out the side of her mouth. "Fine. Like a baby."

He bumped her with his shoulder. "Me too. I think it was the kiss."

She snapped her head to look at him. "I don't know what you're talking about."

"Sure, you don't, but my lips don't lie, and that was some kind of kiss."

"Mediocre at best," she replied.

"Good afternoon, and welcome back to another episode of *The Great Bake Off*. Today is bread day but not any kind of bread. It's quick breads, and since they are supposed to be quick, we thought the bakers could provide us with three each."

Chloe inched toward him. "Do you have the schedule? How did you know?"

He knew she was referring to the quick breads last night. Obviously, she had a memory problem.

"I didn't. Don't forget you were the one with the to-do list. I didn't put quick breads on there."

They had that conversation with no one noticing.

"Oh, right," she said with a sigh.

"Are you going to use my recipe?" He turned to look at her.

"That would be cheating, so no, I'm not."

"The challenge today is to make three quick breads using three different ingredients from the supply table."

Ryan went over the ingredients, but Gage paid no attention. His eyes were on Chloe.

"You can use it. Once I gave it to you, it was fair game. What you do with it is where your talent comes in."

Her facial expression was pinched like she smelled the seaweed Ryan pointed out on the table.

"You have ninety minutes to wow us with your creations. Time starts now."

Isabel, Dwayne, and Lilly took off like sprinters while he and Chloe stared at each other like they were stuck in the blocks. "I'm not using your recipe."

He shrugged. "Suit yourself, but honestly, you're crazy not to. A lot is riding on this competition."

"You don't know what I've got riding on this competition." She spun around and went to the table to grab nuts and dates and raisins. She lifted a handful of herbs and reached for the lemons.

He picked up cranberries and oranges, cloves and cinnamon, and a container of pepper jelly and went back to his station.

He made enough batter for all three.

"Don't forget," he said to Chloe, "It's what you add to it that makes it special."

He watched her dump ingredients into the bowl, but it wasn't his recipe. He understood why she didn't want to use his. She had this sense of propriety, and using his recipe felt wrong to her, but once he told her the recipe, it belonged to her. There were only so many ways to make quick bread.

Ryan moved to Gage's station. "You said it's what you add that makes something special. Tell me about that."

Gage measured cranberries and orange zest and then added orange extract.

"That holds true with anything in life. You can look at a beautiful person, but that might only be skin deep. It's the beauty inside that counts." He lifted the ingredients for the cranberry orange bread. "The basic recipe is the same, but it's what I add to the mix that makes it unique."

"Are you comparing baking to relationships?"

He grated the orange zest into the batter and folded in the cranberries.

"I suppose it's not much different. If you want to win in life, you put your best ingredients forward. Sure, a pretty face is appreciated, but it won't satisfy what you crave if the rest isn't there."

Ryan smiled. "When we released the contestant's pics, your profile got a lot of hits. Are you single?"

He glanced at Chloe, who seemed inattentive, but she inched closer to him as if trying to hear.

"I've got my eyes on someone, and I'm trying to show her what I'm made of inside." He chuckled. "I'm not just a pretty face." He stared into the camera and tried to convey his best boy-next-door look.

"I'm pretty sure you made a few girls swoon."

He turned to his right again. "Let's hope it got to the right girl."

Ryan moved to Isabel and asked her questions. Then, one by one, he included everyone until he rounded back and stood in front of Chloe.

"Chloe Mason, you come from a long line of famous chefs. Why become a pastry chef?"

She visibly winced before her lips turned into a smile.

"Well, Ryan. I'm not a pastry chef. I'm a sous chef and used to work at La Grande Mason and even ran La Petite Mason until my father fired me. When I came to Luxe, they didn't need a sous chef because my sister is the sous chef. They had an opening for a pastry chef, so here I am."

"What do you think your chances of a win are?"

She shrugged. "About the same as there are with the lottery, but I've got a chance, and if I don't play, I can never win."

A screech came from Lilly, and everyone turned to see her open the oven and watch smoke billow out.

"Who turned my oven up?" she yelled. "Someone did, and my bread burned."

A Dollop of Delight

Everyone held their hands up in surrender as if they were the criminals.

Isabel went to her oven, which was next to Dwayne's. "I'm too far away to mess with your oven. Maybe it was Dwayne or Ryan." She laughed. "You have to watch everyone."

Gage took a big breath. This was the second day something untoward happened. Coincidence? He didn't think so.

Since all his bread was done and in the oven, he moved to Lilly's station.

"You want some help?"

She cocked her head in confusion. "You'd help me?"

He didn't see why he shouldn't. "I don't want to win by some mishap. I want the win if I'm truly the best baker. If I got to the end simply because someone dropped their muffins or burned their bread, then what kind of win would that be?"

"A hundred grand win," Dwayne said as he put his pans in the oven.

Gage had never considered Dwayne capable of cheating, but now he wasn't sure. Anyone who put money over everything else was suspect to him.

"Let's do it." He helped Lilly whip up another batch of quick bread. Her recipe was like his, although she used more baking soda and less water.

She used rosemary and mint for one loaf, which was an odd combination, but she swore by it. The other two were more traditional, with a banana nut as one and pumpkin spice as the other.

When Lilly had things under control, he went back to his station to whip up a glaze from orange juice and powdered sugar.

"That was nice," Chloe said.

"Just trying to be a good human."

"An admirable trait." She sprinkled raisins on one loaf and slid it into the oven. When she came back, she glanced down at her workstation.

He looked her way. The stainless steel surface was dusted in flour, and there were bits of seeds and nuts and dried fruit all over.

"How can you work like that?"

"It's controlled chaos."

"Chaos is right."

"Where's your good human now? All you're doing is judging when you could be cleaning."

He chuckled. A look at the timer told him he had five minutes to spare.

"You got it. Put the ingredients away."

She swiped all the containers up, and he rushed over to wash them down.

"Now, you'll have every homemaker in the world in love with you."

"I'm not interested in every homemaker."

She nodded toward the camera. "Don't let them hear you," she whispered. "You'll make the ratings go down."

"Speaking of ratings ..." He turned his back to the camera. "You still don't think that kiss was a ten out of ten?"

He loved it when she blushed. The flood of color rose from her neck and seeped like watercolors into her cheeks.

"You want a rating?"

"Sure. I'd love to know how I compare."

She rolled her eyes. "You don't." Chloe grabbed a bowl from under the counter and dumped in a cup of powdered sugar. Next, she squeezed in the juice of two lemons and stirred before adding chiffonade basil.

"Well, if I had to rate it, I'd give it an eleven."

"Seriously? Only an eleven?" She took out another bowl and made a maple glaze. He knew he needed to get back to his workstation, but the conversation was just getting interesting.

"You didn't even rate it."

"Not true. You asked me how you rated on a scale of one to ten,

A Dollop of Delight

and I said you don't." Her cheeks pinked again. "On that scale, at least." She came close and whispered, "You're a fifteen."

He stumbled back. It was a good shock. His ego took a hit when she said nothing about the kiss that had a real chance of turning into something more. A kiss that said they were more than compatible.

"I'd like to discuss that further, but I need to make some winning glaze for my bread."

Like any baking show, the judges chatted at the table and discussed what they saw going on in the kitchen.

As the time dwindled and oven timers went off, everyone hurried to put their best bread forward.

The hardest part was watching the faces of the three judges tasting your bread and hoping they liked it.

As they deliberated, the five remaining contestants stood like soldiers in the center of the kitchen.

Phillipe Pierre, the French baker, started with Gage and declared his bread to be quick cuisine. He loved everything from the texture to the glaze. Second place went to Isabel, third to Chloe, who got rave reviews from the guest judge but mediocre comments from Phillipe and Gretchen McGraw, who was this decade's Julia Child of the baking world. Fourth was Dwayne, who was visibly upset with his position but thankful to be still in the game.

After they called cut, Paul from security came in and ushered the contestants out of the room. The only people allowed were the stage help, Hildy, Leo, and Ryan.

Gage walked straight to Chloe. "What time do we start work today?"

She glanced at her phone. "We can start now and get off early, or if you need a nap, you can come in later."

He had an excellent idea. "Let's work now, and I'll buy us dinner if we get the job done in time."

"Dinner? Are you asking me out on a date?"

He hadn't considered it a *date* but going out and sharing a meal counted. "Yes, I guess I am."

She giggled. "I can't date my employee."

"Then I quit."

She grabbed a handful of his shirt and tugged him toward the elevator. "Oh, no, you don't. You can quit when the job is done."

"You're a pushy one, aren't you?"

"I'm a Mason. What can I say?"

"Yes, to pizza and beer sometime."

She smiled at him. "We'll see."

Chapter 13

It was getting harder and harder to put Gage off. Nearly every day she saw him, he invited her for coffee, pizza, or a drink. He hadn't tried to kiss her again. While part of her was relieved, the other part was disappointed. She under-exaggerated that kiss by telling him it was a fifteen out of ten. It was more like a twenty. Never had her toes tingled from a kiss. She would've said her shoes were too tight, but she was wearing clogs with a big box toe, so nothing touched them.

Gage was exactly who he seemed to be—a nice person. She couldn't believe how he stepped in to help Lilly, who ended up getting booted that day, anyway. Not because she didn't have quick bread, but because her lemon basil mint bread didn't go over well with the judges.

Two shows had passed since that day, and no significant issues befell anyone.

Today's challenge was cookies, and Chloe went back to her roots. She was a master at cookies because she made them with her grandma Mavis, who favored Italian cookies like anise, pizzelles, and Italian fig cookies.

That was what she was making today—a trio of delight that brought her back to the red-tiled counters in her grandparents' penthouse. Ironically, the place where Allie lived now. It was funny how their lives braided together by fate, or perhaps coincidence. She liked to believe there was a higher power involved. It helped her make sense of the twists and turns her life had taken lately.

The cameras were rolling, and Ryan was hopping from workstation to workstation. He started with Isabel and asked her what cookies she was making.

She grinned for the camera, looking every bit Mrs. Claus. There was no doubt Hildy put her in red for that reason. She was everyone's fantasy of a grandmother.

"Oh, Ryan." She smiled and blushed as if on cue. "I just love the holidays and often wonder why we leave the baking for just a few special occasions during the year." She dumped a pound of butter into the stand mixer, and it started churning. "The key to amazing cookies is love and butter. High-quality ingredients deliver the best taste. Then when you add in a cup of love, you've got a winning recipe."

"You're betting on the win today, right?"

"Everything Grandma makes is a winner."

If Isabel didn't win the baking contest, she'd win the public's hearts. While there was a feeling of unease around the woman, she probably was an excellent baker. There was also the accusation that never sat right with Chloe. Then again, she knew as people got older, they lost their filter. Was it simply that they didn't care how people perceived the message or did they like the shock factor? Even her grandma Mavis had a moment or two when her brain ran behind her lips.

Ryan moved on to Dwayne, who was making something called southern cream cookies. He was also making pralines which wasn't a cookie at all but a candy. Last he had a chocolate chip cookie with pecans that he said would knock the socks off the judges.

Chloe felt like he wasn't taking a risk with a chocolate chip cookie.

"What have you got up your sleeve today?" Gage asked from his spot.

"I'm getting in touch with my inner child and going old school." She mixed the dough for the pizzelles first.

"My grandma Mavis and I used to make all the Christmas and Easter cookies. My father wasn't much into sweets, my mother never touched them, and Gabby preferred savory cooking. Grams and I would spend hours upon hours baking for the family. We'd put together those twine-wrapped pink boxes and deliver cookies around town."

Gage added pecans to his mix and started the churning. "I wonder if it was your grandmother who delivered a box of cookies to my grandparents each year." He stopped the mixer and pulled out the dough.

"It would seem likely. You know ... birds of a feather flock together."

"Speaking of flocking together." He looked around, seeming to make sure the camera wasn't on them. "We aren't working tonight, so after the show, let's hang out."

Each time he asked, her resolve to put distance between them grew weaker.

"Only if you win. That will be your prize." She hated to lose, but deep inside, she hoped she did. Then she could justify the date as part of a bet and not part of her need. She spent far too much time thinking about Gage and how sweet his kiss was.

"You're on."

Ryan swooped in their direction. "Did I hear a wager? A date for a win?"

Chloe snorted. "It's not a date. It's a wager and a free meal."

Blurting that out made her sound like a shrew, but she didn't want her love life broadcast on national television. Though the show wasn't live, she still wanted nothing to drive the attention away from the competition. "I plan to win."

Ryan stood between the two of them. "Tell you what, I say it's a date no matter what, and whoever loses pays. That way, no one goes away empty-handed."

She knew she was being forced into a date with Gage. What better way to drive up ratings and add love into the mix? Who wouldn't love Gage? He was cute and talented, and he kissed like a porn star or what Chloe thought one should kiss like. He helped others around the kitchen and wouldn't stand for anything that resembled cheating. Half the world was already in love with him from his profile on the show's website. When the show went live, he'd make all the ladies swoon. That thought cut like a rusty blade to her heart. Hell, she was half in love with him.

"Deal," she said, without giving it much more thought. "I'm not a cheap date."

He chuckled. "Nor am I."

With something besides the hundred grand to fight for, she made sure the cookies she created today were winners.

Out of the corner of her eye, she watched Gage methodically work on his masterpieces; and they were: pecan caramel shortbread, hidden mint morsels, and strawberry shortcake cookies. They were unique and like works of art when he displayed them on a single, elongated white plate.

She plated the pizzelle in the middle since it was a showstopper and the other cookies on the outside. Her plate was equally impressive, and she knew if everything tasted as magnificent as it looked, the judges would have their work cut out for them. Funny how she didn't take Dwayne or Isabel into consideration for today's competition.

As the baking came to a close, and they lined up in the center of the room like tin soldiers, she halfway hoped she lost.

Chloe hadn't been on a proper date in years. She was a thirty-year-old without a plan. She never aspired to be a shift lead at a resort. From the time she was born, she was groomed to be a chef, not even a sous chef. It was her birthright to take over La Grande Mason, but her father seemed to have different plans.

As the judges tasted and deliberated, she inched toward Gage until their arms skimmed each other.

He turned his head and smiled. She knew he felt that connection, even though she tried to ignore it. The longer they spent in each other's company, the stronger the pull became. For a brief minute, his hand grasped hers, and then Ryan spoke, and the moment was gone. He shifted to his side, putting inches that felt like miles between them.

"Some of you treated the judges to a piece of heaven while others tricked them into thinking you had something special."

He talked to the camera about how there was more at stake than a loss here today. The camera zoomed into their faces.

"Is love on the line too?"

She felt the heat of a familiar blush and hoped her cheeks weren't cherry red.

Gage chuckled. "I know a good thing when I see it. Not only is Chloe beautiful, but she's talented, and she has a good heart. Love on the line? Unlikely if I can't get her on a date."

He smiled, but not at the camera. This smile was for her, and it made her insides tingle.

"One of us has to win."

Isabel made a *pffft* sound. "I plan on winning." She turned to them. "Sorry, kids, you'll have to find love off the set."

"Wait a minute, now. What about me?" Dwayne asked.

"Oh, honey, I'm far too old for you."

"No, I mean, I plan to win."

Isabel waved him off. "Not a chance. You should've stuck with basketball."

He shook his head. "That was the plan, but my knees told a different story."

Ryan loved the interaction because he didn't have to come up with something witty to say. All the banter showed a human side to everyone, which always played well on prime time.

The judges started with Dwayne. Going first never seemed to bode well. They always began with the loser, and when they called his name, he hung his head.

Isabel placed third, which she didn't like. She accused the judges of playing cupid and making sure she or Gage won so they would have the date.

Chloe knew that whoever won deserved it. Their cookies were unique and told a story about their lives. Gage's were little pieces of art and inspiration. Hers were a flashback to better times, a weekend at her grandparents'. While Gage's were filled with inspiration, she filled hers with love.

"Today's winner of *The Great Bake Off* is Chloe Mason, who won the judges over with her pizzelle." Ryan walked to her table where the extras sat and picked one up. "Where's the date going to take place?"

Chapter 14

Gage stood in front of his closet like a teenage boy going on his first date. That's exactly what this felt like. Only he wasn't meeting Sara Rogers at the roller rink. Tonight, he was meeting Chloe at her apartment.

When his phone rang, he jumped several inches into the air.

He pulled the phone from his back pocket.

"What's up?" His sister had called earlier and left a message about meeting at her house to watch the first episode of *The Great Bake Off*.

"Are you coming? Mom is springing for a pizza, and I made your favorite cookies."

Any cookie was his favorite cookie.

"Sorry, I can't." Did he dare tell her he had a date? Anything less would have her strong-arming him into showing up, but a date would shut her up.

"What do you mean you can't? Anything short of a hot date is unacceptable."

It was funny how she pressured him, but she'd given up on dating when Jesse was born. He imagined having the father of your child abandon you did something to a girl's ego, but each time he told his sister to get back in the saddle, she gave him a million reasons why it wasn't wise.

"Then I guess my excuse is acceptable."

The squeal coming from the other end made his ears ring.

"You have a date? What's her name? Is she pretty? What does she do?"

"Do you think jeans are too casual?"

"Gage! I need information. How am I supposed to live vicariously through you if I don't have the details?"

"You're not supposed to live through me, but instead, have your own life. Wouldn't it be wonderful to have someone to depend on? Jesse could use a good role model."

"He has you. Now tell me before I twist an ankle from jumping up and down."

He knew the exact moment she sat because her chair always squeaked. It was on his list of honey-do items to fix. It wasn't easy being the only man in the family.

"It's Chloe from the show."

Silence filled the air. "That little blonde girl?"

Knowing his sister, she probably had files on all the contestants.

"She's a grown woman, but yes, Chloe is blonde." He stayed in his jeans and wore a button-down shirt.

"She's that girl whose family is famous in Aspen for their culinary skills, right?"

"Yep, the Masons have a reputation." He wouldn't tell her the stuff he'd heard because Courtney was fiercely loyal, and that would jade her opinion.

"Is she still competing? Are you?"

One of the contract requirements was you couldn't discuss the show outside of the set. He had privileged information that could ruin the experience for others.

"You know I can't tell you."

"Are you allowed to date someone competing in the show?" She was fishing for information.

"You can't be related to someone affiliated with the show, that's a no, but there isn't a rule against dating."

She made a *harrumph* sound. "You're no fun."

"You've never dated me."

"That would be gross and probably illegal." She stalled for a moment. "Wear jeans and a button-down. You don't want to dress up too much because showing her how desperate you are for a date puts her in a position of power. The jeans and nice shirt are a good mix."

"I don't want to look like a bum."

She laughed. "You'll be a well-dressed bum. Where are you taking her?"

"We're going to her place. Probably do the same as you and mom. Order a pizza and see how ridiculous we look on TV."

"You can bring her over." There was a hint of hope in her voice.

"Not on a first date. Should I pick up flowers?" He heard his mom's voice in his head. *"Go nowhere empty-handed."*

"Yes, definitely flowers."

"Okay, give Jesse a hug."

"I want all the juicy gossip in the morning."

He rested the phone between his ear and shoulder while he buttoned his shirt.

"You've got the wrong guy, sis. I never kiss and tell."

"Again. No fun."

She hung up before he could respond.

At his feet, Sassy made figure eights around his legs. "Hey, Sass, what do you think?" He moved in a circle to show her every angle. "Will I do?"

She rubbed her head against his ankle as if to say, yes, he'd do in a pinch.

He beat the cat to the kitchen, which he never did, but he was excited about the date. He'd only had a single kiss, and it would never be enough. Chloe knew how to crush a man's ego and build him back up to feeling like a god by telling him that his kiss didn't rank ... because it was off the charts.

He fixed Sassy's evening meal, scratched her behind the ears, and left. Funnily enough, Chloe lived nearby the bakery. They were practically neighbors. The only thing between them was a mile of sidewalk.

Outside, the sun was setting, and the sky was glowing a bright orange. Wisps of clouds floated by on a breeze, carrying with it the scent of pine and something that smelled like pasta sauce.

He strolled into the store on the corner and picked through their flowers. He didn't want roses because they said love.

"Can I help you?" The clerk was a young woman of Chloe's age.

"Umm, yes. If I'm bringing flowers to a first date, what do you suggest?"

She scratched her head and smiled. "Is it a get lucky date?"

Was it? While he would never turn down the offer of a "get lucky" date with Chloe, that's not what this was. It was a normal date.

"No, it's the first date."

She waved him off. "Skip the roses and grab the mixed bunch. It leaves you options."

He paid for the flowers and continued on his way, but he wondered if there was a list of flowers that meant something. He knew red roses were for love, but what did a daisy say?

Before he even realized it, he was there. Just as he raised his hand to knock, the door swung open, and Chloe stood dressed in jeans and a button-down shirt nearly identical to his, but the blue was brighter.

He pointed to his shirt. "I got the memo on the uniform."

She giggled. It was a light trill that pleased his ears. "You've got excellent taste in fashion." She moved to the side. "Come on in."

He stepped inside and thrust the flowers forward. "These are for you."

"You brought me flowers?"

"Seems the right thing to do for a first date."

A snort came out with her laugh. "Seems like we were roped into it. Ratings will go up if they can add in romance."

Before she could take the flowers, he snapped them back. "If you don't want them, I'll bring them home to my girl. She prefers dandelions, but she's not too picky."

She snatched them from his hand. "You have a girl, and you're out with me?"

"Yes, she's twelve pounds of feline attitude, and if she eats the flowers, she gifts me by choking up a few hairballs."

She brought the flowers to her nose and inhaled.

He'd done the same on the way over, but all he smelled was earth.

"They're lovely. Tell your female suitor she'll have to find another date for the evening. You're mine."

Those two words rushed straight through him, leaving a warm feeling buzzing in his veins. He liked the idea of being hers but didn't want to make the moment awkward by saying so.

"What do I smell?" He lifted his nose in the air and breathed deeply.

She moved to the stove and stirred whatever was in the pot. "This is heaven." She dipped the spoon back in and came out with red sauce. "Taste it."

He blew on the steaming spoon and flicked his tongue out to test the temperature. When he was sure it wouldn't blister his mouth, he wrapped his lips around the utensil and savored the taste of garlic and tomatoes and basil.

"You're right. It's amazing."

Chloe rarely smiled on the show. Her face was always set in a stern, have-to-win expression, so her broad smile was a treat. It's not that he hadn't caught glimpses or that she never smiled, but she was mostly serious as if her life depended on the win.

"It was my grandma Mavis's recipe. She slow-cooked Roma tomatoes, garlic, and Italian spices. Her secret was the Italian sausage she crumbled up so finely that it became part of the sauce. That and freshly grated parmesan."

"I could've brought dessert."

She glanced at a recipe book on her counter. "I thought we'd make cupcakes together before the show starts."

He took a stool at her island and pulled the book to him. *Recipes for Love*.

When he went to flip the page, she said, "No. It has to be that recipe."

He put the page back to Kiss Me Cupcakes.

"Why this recipe?"

Her cheeks pinked. "I let the cookbook choose for me." She looked at the ceiling and shook her head. "Call me crazy, but I'm a rule follower, and the rules of this book say you're only allowed to pick one recipe and then pass it on."

"And if you don't follow the rule? What then?"

She shrugged. "I don't know, but I don't want to test fate. I don't need any bad juju in my life. If I'm going to win the competition, I need all the positive energy I can muster."

Like him, she hadn't entered the competition, but also like him, it was essential for her to win. What was at stake?

"Tell me, Ms. Mason. Why is the win so important to you?"

She plated up two pasta dishes, and as if by magic, she pulled garlic bread from the oven and a salad from the refrigerator.

She took the seat next to him and twirled spaghetti on her fork. "My sense of self is riding on this win."

"What do you mean?"

She turned toward him, and in between bites, she explained her situation and how she was always picked second. Second daughter. Second place. Second choice. "He even released my inheritance so I could spend it on La Petite Mason. When I refused to update the kitchen with the money my grandparents left me, he fired me and blacklisted me from every worthwhile restaurant in Aspen. The only job I could get was as the baking lead at Luxe."

"Were you a baker?"

She smiled. "I worked in French restaurants all my life and have had some training, but I'm not a pastry chef." She mopped up the sauce on her plate with the bread and took a bite.

While she chewed, he thought about how that betrayal must have felt. The joy of being chosen to get the restaurant only to find out her father was using her to spend her inheritance.

While his father was hard on him, he never used him. He may not have bubbled with pride, but Gage always felt loved. His family's problem was that they were so steeped in tradition that they hadn't moved on with the times. People didn't want hot cross buns. They wanted raspberry rum and margarita cupcakes.

"You seem to do well in your current position."

She forked a tomato and brought it toward her mouth. "I had to make a Chantilly cake for my interview." She ate the tomato and continued. "I mean, I had the job, but it was Allie's birthday, and I was certain I'd get fired if it wasn't perfect, so I dove right into it. I gained four pounds, testing out my homemade Chantilly cakes until I perfected it. Then I tested cupcakes on the buffet, hoping to find which one appealed the most to the guests."

"Which was it?"

"None really. I hadn't perfected the recipe." She tapped the book. "But this recipe is to die for."

"And you're going to share it with me?"

"You shared your quick bread recipe, which, by the way, is a favorite on the breakfast buffet. We'll need to up our production to keep up with demand."

"I'm glad I'm contributing something positive." He touched his chin. "I've been wondering, if given the chance, would you go back to work for your father?"

She didn't even take a breath before she answered. "As crazy as it seems, the answer is yes. If he offered me a restaurant again without all the strings attached to my inheritance, I'd jump at it."

He couldn't believe his ears. "Why when you have that history with him?"

She hemmed and hawed for a moment. "I don't know if I can explain it, but it's kind of like when an actress takes a role she hates just to be in a movie some difficult but legendary director is making. It might be hell, but the experience is worth the hassle. No one can elevate my career faster than my father. He's connected in every way possible. He knows people, and his people know people. His influence is far-reaching. Better work for him than against him."

He understood what she meant. It might not have been right, but family ties ran deep. He couldn't imagine the pressure if those ties could control your future with a phone call.

When she finished, he gathered her plate. If she cooked, he'd clean.

"I'll take care of the mess."

"I've got it." He lifted his chin toward the cookbook. "Gather the ingredients. I like the idea of Kiss Me Cupcakes if there is going to be kissing after we finish them."

She moved to the cupboard. "Oh, there's definitely going to be kissing. Didn't you read the cover? This is a recipe for love."

Chapter 15

"Why are you so neat about everything? Baking is like fingerpainting. You never know what the masterpiece will be if you don't let your imagination run wild."

Every little spill Chloe made, Gage wiped up.

"It's a learned behavior. My father ran the bakery like a drill sergeant runs his troops."

"That had to be hard."

"It was very confining."

Her rebellious streak took over. Her hand slipped inside the flour bag to grab a handful, and when she pulled it out, she tossed it into the air, creating a shower of white powder.

"You didn't." He reached for her, but she took off with a cloud of flour floating behind her.

"I did." She laughed so hard she had to stop and grab her stomach. "You should see your face."

He came after her, but she kept a piece of furniture between them. First, it was the couch, and then she went back to the kitchen and ran around the island while he chased her.

She'd regret this tomorrow. Though she was a messy baker, she was a tidy housekeeper.

"You know I'm going to catch you."

She giggled. "I know, but the question is, what will you do when that happens?"

He slowed down on his side of the island. "I'm going to kiss the brat out of you."

She stopped moving. "In that case, come and get me."

They were both dusted in white, from their hair to their shoes.

He moved toward her like a predator. He slinked slowly in her direction. She was sure he was testing to see if she'd run, but she craved his kisses. That one in the server station wasn't enough.

"You're a mess," he said when he stood before her. He cupped her cheeks and brushed the flour from them with his thumbs. "But a beautiful mess." His lips grazed hers in a tease. He stepped back and smiled.

"I'm not the only mess." She ruffled his hair and sent a dusting of flour back into the air. "But … you're a beautiful mess too." She lifted on tiptoes and kissed him. Not the innocent brush on the lips like his but a full-on, tongue battling, breath halting kiss. When she pulled away, she felt invigorated and filled with energy.

"Wow," he said. "Totally off the charts."

"I agree, and we haven't even baked the cupcakes yet." She stepped back. "I made a mess of you." The poor man had flour in his ears, up his nose, and the creases by his neck. "You want to shower?"

His eyes grew wide. "Are you inviting me to get naked with you?"

Why her cheeks had to heat each time something sensual came up, she didn't know. It wasn't like she was a virgin. She'd given that up a long time ago to an actual French chef who worked for her father. She'd heard French men were supposed to be great lovers, but Peter was nothing to write home about.

"No, I'm offering you my shower. If you give me your clothes, I think a toss in the dryer should be sufficient until you get home and do your laundry."

He glanced down at jeans that looked more stonewashed than the indigo he wore into the house. His once blue shirt was the color of a pale sky.

"I think that might be wise, but let me help with the cupcakes first."

They worked side by side on the cupcakes. It was the plain batter, but she pulled out all the preserves she had, and they filled them with various flavors.

Once they were in the oven and the timer set, she showed him the bathroom and stood by the door, waiting for his clothes.

At the laundry room, she realized he didn't have a towel because they were all in the dryer. Maybe if she were quiet, she could sneak one in.

When she arrived at the bathroom door, she second-guessed going in without him knowing, so she knocked.

"Yes," he called from the shower.

"Umm, I have a towel for you."

He told her to come in.

She held the towel to her chest as she walked into the steamy bathroom. Her apartment wasn't high-end by any means, but she had a nice shower with multiple jets. It was her one guilty pleasure. After a long day on her feet hefting trays of baked goods and mixer bowls full of batter, she liked to stand in the shower and let the pulsing water massage her sore body.

"Where do you want it?" The steam swirled around, giving her glimpses of his shadow. What she saw was like icing on the cake. He was handsome and nice, and the outline of his body was oh so delicious.

"Anywhere."

She didn't want to set the towel down and dash when the view was so good. After a moment of silence, she realized he'd shut off the water and stood with the door open—full-frontal nudity.

"You gonna stand there and stare?"

If she thought her cheeks heated before, she felt them flame and burn right then.

"Oh my, I'm sorry."

He smiled. "Don't be." He took the towel from her and wrapped it around his waist. "That is the best shower I've ever been in. I think I might shower here every day."

Mesmerized by his presence, she nodded. "I'd like that."

He smiled, and she was sure it was as bright as the ray of sunshine that peeked through her blinds each morning.

"I should go."

He reached for her hand and tugged her back. "Oh, no, you don't." He pointed to the shower. "Your turn. You shower, and I'll watch the cupcakes."

She caught sight of herself in a sliver of mirror that hadn't fogged. "Look at me. I'm a wreck."

"You're beautiful." He leaned forward and touched his lips to hers without touching another part of her body. "I'll find the dryer and bring you a towel." He reached for the one at his waist. "Or you can have this one."

"No, that's okay, I'll get one." She ran from the bathroom to the laundry room, with Gage following a step behind.

"You don't have to run from me."

"I'm not. I'm just..." She wiped her face. "I'm so embarrassed. I stared at you."

"Tell you what. I'll bring you a towel and do the same."

She gasped. "You will not." She pulled his clothes from the dryer, and they were indeed flour-free. "You get dressed and watch the cupcakes."

She pressed his clothes to his chest, grabbed a clean towel, and raced to the bathroom. While she showered, she kept one eye on the door, thinking Gage might sneak in. When she finished and dressed in clean clothes, half of her was relieved he didn't, and half was disappointed.

"Those smell so good." She padded barefoot into the kitchen to find Gage mixing the buttercream frosting. She had to laugh because he'd whipped her kitchen back into shape in no time at all. No one would be the wiser to their flour fight.

He looked at the cookbook again. "This Adelaide Phelps lady knows how to whip up a batch of love." He ran his finger around the edge of the bowl and touched it to her lips. Without a second thought, she sucked the frosting off. That action seemed more intimate than the kiss they shared earlier. "Oh, that's good."

"Can't go wrong with butter and powdered sugar, but it's the heavy cream and lemon juice that makes it magical."

She dipped her finger into the bowl and pulled out a dollop.

"It's like crack. I could sit here and eat this whole bowl without the cupcakes."

He pointed to the perfectly baked cupcakes cooling on the counter. "They need frosting love too." He picked up one cupcake and swirled a layer of frosting on top. "Besides, Adelaide promises these are the way to the heart." He set the cupcake down and picked another up to frost.

"No, she says that love is like baking and should be done with passion."

He lifted his eyes, and she swore there was an inferno fired up behind them. "Maybe I should slather you with frosting."

"Next time," she teased. "Right now, we have naked cupcakes and a show to watch." She placed the finished cupcakes on a plate with shaky hands. "How ridiculous do you think we'll look?"

"Best looking couple on TV."

"Are we a couple?"

He gave her a quick kiss on the lips. "I like you ... a lot."

"Why?" It was an odd question to ask, but she needed to know.

He took the plate of cupcakes from her hand and led her to the living room. "You want a list?"

She took a seat, and he sat beside her.

"A few bullet points might be nice." She hated the insecure feeling she got with men, but her role models were lacking. All she had was her father, who didn't like or respect her as a person. He only appreciated her when she brought something positive to his table.

"Let's start with the obvious."

She waited for him to tell her she was pretty.

"You're talented."

She didn't expect that. "Is that all?" She smiled.

"Not by far." He picked up a cupcake and held it to her lips. When she took a bite and got fig, she hummed. "Like this cupcake, you're full of surprises. You try to be hard on the outside, but your soft sweet center shows through."

"Okay."

He shook his head. "Oh, I'm not finished. You kiss like a goddess and smell like a candy shop, and you taste better than Adelaide's crack frosting. Besides, you have a great shower." He turned to face the television. "And your television is bigger than mine."

She snorted. "You have television envy."

"And shower envy."

"Tell me how this Kiss Me Cupcake works." She took the treat from his hand and set it on the plate.

"I think you're supposed to taste one. It's some bakery voodoo or something."

"How about I just kiss you first?"

She leaned into him. "I don't think those are the rules, but okay. I'm game to twist things up a bit."

His mouth was on hers, and he tasted like everything she'd ever craved in her life. Their tongues tangled. His hands threaded through her hair and held her in place like he was afraid she'd disappear.

She'd never been kissed the way Gage kissed her. When he pulled away, she could still feel the energy of the kiss linger on her lips. If he continued to make love to her lips the way he did, she wasn't going anywhere ... ever.

"Shall we embarrass ourselves?"

She snuggled into his side and turned on the television.

"Look at you," he said, pointing to the TV when they lined up in the kitchen to be introduced by Ryan. "You're so cute."

"I look like I'm ready to kill someone."

He squeezed her. "That's your competition face."

"Do I look so serious all the time?"

He rocked his head back and forth. "No, sometimes you look like you want to kill me instead of kiss me."

She growled. "When you threw me under the bus, I wanted to murder you."

"I didn't throw you. That was Isabel."

"True, but you didn't defend me either."

He picked her up and pulled her into his lap. "And for that, I'll apologize. But in my defense, I hadn't kissed you and didn't know what I was missing."

She nibbled at his lower lip, setting aside the growing irritation that came with thinking about that day.

"Do you think someone is sabotaging the show?"

"You want to talk about that, or do you want to kiss?"

"Kiss, all I want is your kisses."

He bit her lip and let it pop free from his teeth. "Baby, you might want to rethink that. There's so much more to me than kisses."

She buried her head against his shoulder. "I know. I may have peeked while you showered."

He laughed. "Chloe, that wasn't peeking. You open-mouth gawked at me."

"It was hard to breathe in there from all the steam."

"Yeah, sure. If that's what you tell yourself."

"It's what I'm going with now until I come up with a better excuse."

He kissed her again, slowly, then pulled away. "There's no reason we can't indulge."

She thought of a bunch, starting with him working for her and ending with him being her closest competition.

"Overindulging will give you a bellyache."

"Then let's enjoy until we feel a little queasy." He kissed her again, and she was lost in those lips. Lips that made her forget about all the obstacles standing in their way. When Gage kissed her, everything felt possible. But was it?

Chapter 16

"Did you get naked?" Courtney asked.

"Yes, I did." He smirked because he knew exactly where his sister's head was at.

"You gloved it before you loved it, right?" She leaned forward to whisper. "Otherwise, you might end up like me."

Gage didn't know why she was whispering. They were the only two people in the bakery. Mom was getting her hair styled, and Jesse was in school.

"First off, I'm teasing you. You should know that I never kiss and tell."

Disappointment settled in her blue-gray eyes. She had their father's eyes. Eyes that pierced your skin and saw into your soul.

"Second, while I may have gotten naked, it was to shower and not for sex. We had a flour fight."

"What are you, a ten-year-old?"

"Last night, I felt like a kid. It was nice to let all the stress of adulting go and have a little fun."

"You don't get to be a kid when you have one."

His sister's life wasn't easy, but it wasn't unbearable either.

She had a good support system and everything she needed, except companionship.

"I wouldn't say your life is all that awful."

"Do you know how many accounting gigs I have to take on to keep that kid in athletic shoes?"

"Just be grateful you're not depending on the bakery for your full support."

She let her shoulders roll forward. "I shouldn't be taking any of it. Honestly, it barely makes enough to support one family but has the burden of helping three. That's a heavy weight to bear."

It was why they were at the bakery that morning. They were taking inventory of what they could sell if the bakery closed.

"The refrigeration units are newer," she said. "We could probably get several thousand for each of them, and the building is worth something."

Their parents owned the building, but it needed some work. Mostly it was cosmetic, but if he won the competition, he'd have the cash to turn the place around. A hundred grand went a long way when you provided a lot of the labor.

"I can't believe Dad left Mom with nothing but the bakery."

He sighed. "I know. Dad seemed the type who had it all figured out and planned. I've tried to keep it open, but their business model doesn't work, and Mom is as stubborn as Dad."

Courtney leaned on the freezer. "Well, he's not here, and she can't continue to live in the past."

Gage looked up. "I can't help but feel like he's watching me. He was so hard on me and discounted all my ideas. It was always his way or the highway."

"He wasn't a pleasant man."

That was an understatement. Martin Sweet ran this shop like a military general, and his family members were the soldiers. It was why Gage was so tidy when he baked. His father would've beaten his ass if he'd worked like Chloe. Part of him wondered if

A Dollop of Delight

Chloe went out of her way to be messy as a sign of rebellion. After talking to her last night, he realized their fathers were similar. Hers might have been more devious, but they both demanded and got what they wanted. They ruled with an iron fist. Though they were alike in their parentage, their need for the win wasn't similar at all. Hers wasn't tied to survival. Not physically, at least. Hers was a father versus self battle while his was a need for shelter and food for his family and cans of smelly goodness for Sassy.

"Don't you have a competition to win today?"

He glanced down at his phone. "I should go, but I don't want to leave you here to inventory everything."

She waved him off. "Bring home the hundred grand."

"You know, I've only won one of three competitions, right?" As soon as he said it, he cupped his hand over his mouth. "You didn't hear that."

"Oh, my goodness, which one?" She danced in place.

"Court, I'm in breach of contract as it is. Spilling the beans can remove me from the contest."

She deflated like bread without enough yeast.

"Okay, we can't afford for you to get disqualified, so I promise not to tell, but I bet it was for your cupcakes."

At the mention of cupcakes, he thought of the ones they made last night. He would've thought a standard batter was simply that —standard, but Adelaide Phelps's cupcakes changed his world. Or maybe it was the girl he ate them with.

"We haven't made cupcakes yet." That was a safe enough subject.

"You're totally going to win." She scrunched her nose. "I hope that Lilly lady and the guy from Levity don't win. They don't need the money. Their companies are doing fine. And that basketball player probably made more in a year than we will in a lifetime. The granny seems nice. Then there's your girlfriend. You probably should've held off developing a relationship until after the show ended. What happens if you two are the last two standing?"

He started toward the door. "It's the last three standing, and we'll handle that situation when it comes. I'm not borrowing trouble."

"But we need this so badly."

"I know we do." He kissed his sister's forehead and walked out the door. The weight of the world sat heavily on his shoulders. He headed to his car, wishing he was back in Chloe's kitchen getting doused by flour. It may have been a childish act, but he loved the spontaneity and that she could play around and not take things too seriously. He hoped if he won the contest that they could still pursue what they'd started.

"Hey, Muffin Girl," he said when he walked into the set kitchen.

Chloe spun around to face him. "Hey, Hot Buns." Her smile was as sparkly and bright as a flawless diamond.

"Girl." He shook his head. "You have no idea if my buns are hot." He looked around to make sure no one was within hearing distance. "Your eyes were laser-focused on my other finer parts." Teasing her was fun because of the crimson color bleeding into her cheeks.

"I focused my eyes on the puddle of water you left on my floor."

"Hardly, but if that's how you want to play it, okay."

She brushed past him, making sure her body slid against his. All the nerve endings she touched on the way lit up, and a smoldering fire heated him from the inside out. This woman was trouble.

"They said to grab what we need from the pantry."

"How do we know what we need?" He looked at Isabel and Dwayne, who had armfuls of supplies. "What did I miss?"

She shrugged. "Didn't your parents tell you that on time was late and early was on time? Or the early bird gets the worm?"

He watched the packets of yeast line up on Isabel's station. She also had nuts and seeds.

"Are we making bread?"

Chloe shrugged and walked past him.

"You're not telling me?" He couldn't believe that she'd leave him out of the loop.

She gathered an armful of ingredients. "I'm helping you get caught up." She looked over her shoulder at her table, which was neat as a pin. It was so tidy that even his father would've been proud. "There are two contests where we know what we're making. Today Leo came in and said 'bread,' then turned out and walked away."

"What's the second one?"

"They haven't told us." She dumped the standard bread ingredients on his table. "You want them in order of use or alphabetized?"

He knew she was teasing. "Now you're a comedian?" He gathered the items she'd brought and put them in order of use. It was how he worked. Doing it this way made mistakes less likely.

"Why do you show up at the last minute?"

It was a habit he'd picked up. The earlier he was to work, the more he had to listen to his father.

"I stopped by the bakery to help my sister, Courtney, with the inventory. If this gig doesn't pay off, we're going to sell the bakery."

She stopped to gawk at him, and her jaw went slack. "But that place has been in your family for decades."

"You can't make bread without flour ... good bread anyway, and you can't run a bakery without money."

"Are things that dire?"

He looked away from her. He wasn't the type to whine about his situation. Lots of people dealt with hardships.

"It's all good." It wasn't good. Things were dire, but he wouldn't tell her he was two months behind on the electric and he owed their distributor for the last delivery. Working at Luxe would bring him some money, and hopefully, he could pay on both accounts to keep everyone off his back.

"Are you sure?"

"What's our schedule at Luxe this week?"

"Off today and on tomorrow after the filming of the show."

"Right." He knew the schedule, but changing the subject avoided the pressing questions.

Ryan walked on to the set with the makeup artist scurrying behind him, waving a puffball.

"Take your spot because we're on in two." He leaned over and let the girl powder the shine from his nose before turning to Chloe. "We'll lead with your date."

She opened her mouth to talk, but the director counted down. "We're live in five, four, three, two, one."

"Welcome back to *The Great Bake Off* where things can really heat up in the kitchen." He walked the length of the set and stood to Chloe's side. Though her upper body remained still, her right foot tapped nervously on the ground. "We're down to four. Sadly, we had to say goodbye to Lilly and then Matt. Vying for the win and the hundred thousand dollars are Dwayne, Isabel, Gage, and Chloe."

The camera panned the contestants. They were used to smiling for film. On their first day, Hildy came in and gave them a lesson. He understood why after seeing last night's first episode air. Poor Chloe had her jaw set so hard he was sure she had a toothache the whole night from all the clenching and grinding she must have done. Hildy said too small a smile, and you look unpleasant or constipated, and too big a smile, and you were a buffoon. Her words, not his.

"So, Chloe." He moved to her side. "Do you think there's a recipe for love?"

He watched her clench her teeth, and as if remembering Hildy's words, her lips twisted then fell into a soft smile.

"Oh, I don't know. Some traits make someone easy to fall in love with, like honesty, kindness, integrity. Those were ingredients I'd look for when searching for love."

Ryan moved to Gage. "What about you? What would be in your recipe for love?"

"Sacrifice and commitment. You have to have a measure of both to make things work. My parents were married for over thirty years before my father passed away, and I think it worked because they knew when to give and when to take."

Ryan walked to Isabel. "You've got some experience on these young ones surrounding you. What's the secret ingredient to long-term love?"

Isabel rubbed at her eyes. "I sure miss my Henry. He was a good man." She played with the cameo pin on her chest. "My grandmother Esther, God rest her soul, told me the secret to a long-lasting relationship was knowing how to pick your battles. Henry and I never fought, so I never got to use her advice, but it sounded wise."

"What about you, Dwayne?" Ryan tilted his head back to look at the man who was well over six feet tall.

"Prenup. That's all I'm saying."

This was where they would dub in audience laughter.

"If you tuned in to our last episode, we had a wager, and Chloe won, which put her on a date with Gage." He hustled back to Chloe. "How was the date?"

"It wasn't a date. We had pasta and made cupcakes."

Gage laughed. "We also had a food fight."

Chloe gasped. "It wasn't a food fight. It was a flour fight." She swiped up a handful of flour and tossed it into the air. The fans caught it and sent it into the other contestants. Within minutes, there was an all-out war, and by the time the director yelled cut, white covered all four contestants and Ryan.

"That will get us some ratings," Leo said. "Now, let's get cleaned up. You've got bread to bake."

Isabel refused to help with the cleanup. She said she was too old to play games and at her age was too old to be punished for them. One of the stagehands, feeling sorry for her, took her place in the cleanup.

Three hours later and Gage was named the winner of the bread challenge. In all honestly, if he hadn't won, he might as well have packed it up. You can't come from a bread-making family and not know how to make bread. He could only imagine his father rolling over in his grave if he had lost. At least, this time, he wouldn't have been a total disappointment.

Chapter 17

Her dad had left two messages already, but Chloe refused to answer them. He would've heard about the show and no doubt wanted to chastise her for embarrassing the family.

"Wait until he sees the flour fight episode."

"What was that?" Kinsley asked.

Chloe had stopped in the locker room to drop off her bag and jacket. There wasn't anywhere else to store stuff. She'd also brought in the leftover cupcakes she and Gage had made two nights ago.

"I can't talk about it, but if you're watching the baking show, episode five has some shenanigans."

"What did you do?"

Chloe placed her hand over her chest. "Moi?" She stepped back as if someone had slapped her. "Why would you think I did anything?"

"Because I know you."

A giggle slipped past her lips. Kinsley knew she had a wicked side. It was probably all the years she had to toe the line that she was making up for. She was known for practical jokes like cutting out the bottoms of Styrofoam cups. Nothing that would cause undue stress, but since Kinsley had a teenage boy, she could appreciate the prank and often repeated them on her son and sometimes Julian, who was far too serious; it was the way of bean counters and accountants. In her experience, they didn't have much of a sense of humor.

"I started a food fight of sorts." She buttoned her lip. "But you never heard that from me."

"Is that your way of getting back at Allie for making you compete?"

She hadn't thought of it, but she was rebelling against something each time she reverted to a six-year-old.

"No, it was my way of getting the host to stop asking about Gage and me."

Kinsley sat on the locker room bench, tugging on her work shoes.

"Oooh," she cooed. "Is there a you and Gage? That kiss in the server area was almost pornographic." She tied her shoes and sat up straight. "I have to say he's cute, but won't there be a conflict of interest?"

"Totally. I'd give up the win for another one of his kisses any day."

"Seriously? Only a kiss." She stood and tied the black apron around her waist. "I, of all people, know that you have to set your expectations high, especially when it comes to yourself."

Kinsley had been through a lot with her dead ex-husband, who was an idiot. She asked for little and got less.

"I have no expectations. All I can say is when he came over the other night, I saw what I could expect, and it was a lot bigger than I could've hoped for."

"He came over? You had a date, and you didn't call your bestie?"

"I was busy kissing him and holding his towel while he showered."

She picked up her phone and frowned. "You should've come out of the gate with that. I mean, now I have to go to work, and I won't get any details."

Chloe shoved her things into her locker. "There aren't many details. We made some cupcakes from a recipe book I found in my locker."

"You did?" Kinsley's eyes opened wide. "Did he eat them?"

Chloe caught on to the rise in excitement. "What do you know about that cookbook?"

Kinsley shook her head. "Nothing, but make sure you follow the rules. No cheating." She rushed toward the door.

"Kinsley, you're in trouble."

Kinsley stopped at the doorframe and laughed. "If you both ate those cupcakes, you're the one in trouble."

Chloe slammed her locker and chased after Kinsley. "What do you know?"

Kinsley stopped. "I know that you'll be late if you don't hurry."

She looked at the clock in the kitchen. If she didn't hurry, she'd break her own rules of timeliness.

She raced to the conference room and her station.

"Running late, Muffin Girl?" Gage was already standing in place in the center of the kitchen. The makeup girl raced over to Chloe. "You're a mess. Let me help you out."

"I'm a mess?" She stepped back and looked at Gage. "Do I look a mess?"

"You're a beautiful mess." He blew her a kiss that made the makeup artist swoon.

"If you don't nab him, a million viewers will." She pressed a compact applicator against Chloe's face. The girl named Sadie then pulled a lip gloss out of her apron pocket. "Let me pretty you up."

Chloe waved her hands in front of her face. She wasn't much for makeup or making a fuss over how she looked. "Did he get lip gloss and face powder?" She nodded toward Gage.

"No, he's perfect the way he is."

She opened her mouth to complain. "Seriously—"

"Chloe," a familiar voice bellowed, and all the life drained out of her. "Let the girl pretty you up. Show the world that the Masons have beauty and talent."

Her father's voice slithered over her skin like a snake, all scaly and cold and unwelcome.

"What are you doing here?" Her voice didn't sound like the woman she was, but the child her father made her feel like.

"Leo is a friend of a friend, and when I called and asked if I could watch the taping, he said yes. You know, it's hard to say no to a Mason."

It wasn't hard, but Chloe knew few people did. To say no was like poking an angry bear when you were tied in its cave. There wasn't a place to run and hide that her father couldn't find you or get to you.

"What are you doing here?" she repeated. He didn't come to cheer her on. That wasn't his style.

"I saw the show last night. You really should smile." He moved toward her and kissed her cheek like a normal father would. "Why didn't you tell me you were competing?"

"Because it didn't involve you."

He clucked with his tongue. "Not true. You're a Mason, and we're a brand. Everything you do involves me."

"We're filming in three minutes," the director shouted.

"You need to go." Chloe shuffled back. "I need to focus. You're a distraction."

Her father pointed to the corner. "I'll be right over there. After, I thought we'd meet for a late lunch or early dinner."

A Dollop of Delight

She shook her head hard enough to rattle her brains. "Sorry, I have to work."

Gage saw her distress and watched her father like a hawk did its prey.

"Mr. Mason," Gage stepped forward. "I'm a huge fan."

As soon as her father smiled and opened his mouth to speak, Gage continued. "Of your daughter. She's an amazing baker and a talented chef."

Her father's smile morphed into a thin line. She saw him trying to read Gage like a book, but he didn't quite get the connection between the competitors. In any other world, she would've never befriended someone who could take the win from her. That was how she was raised, but she was living her own life, and all those warnings went out the window the day Gage kissed her.

"And you are?" Michael Mason asked.

"I'm no one."

"In five, four, three," the director shouted, and her father moved into the shadows.

Gage ran back to his spot before the filming started.

Ryan stood next to the judges and chatted on camera, which gave Chloe a moment to regain her composure.

"Thanks for the save. You didn't have to lie, though."

"Everything I said was the truth. I'm a huge fan of yours."

She was filled with warm happiness that blanketed the cold her father left behind.

Ryan moved dead center, splitting Gage and her from Isabel and Dwayne.

"We're down to four, and today we'll find out who stays on top and who sinks to the bottom." He paused for a second. "It's souffle day. This isn't Cupcake Wars. It's not Ace of Cakes. This show highlights all facets of baking, and the winner has to stand the heat from the kitchen." He moved like Michael Jackson doing the moonwalk to the side of the set. "Today, we're comparing apples to apples, and every baker has to make a chocolate souffle and a cheese souffle. What you do with them is up to you, but you only have an hour to create both. Ready, get set, go."

Chloe gathered her ingredients. If there was one thing she could make, it was a souffle. Her grandfather was world-renowned for them, and she was pretty sure she knew how to bake one before she was fully potty trained.

"You got this?" Gage asked as he combined his ingredients.

"I can make one in my sleep." Her eyes gravitated toward her father, who scowled at her when she picked up the can of already-grated parmesan cheese. She had to cut corners if she was going to make two souffles in an hour, but that look brought her back to a thousand memories, and her muscles wouldn't behave.

"Bring it on."

She glanced at her father once more.

"Fine," she grumbled and ran to the refrigeration unit where she knew she'd find fresh parmesan she could grate.

"Getting fancy there, Muffin Girl?" Gage asked.

"Stop calling me that." She grated the cheese and lined ramekins with butter before sprinkling them with the fresh Parmigiano Reggiano.

"I could call you hot lips instead," he said.

"And I could find something equally embarrassing to call you."

"Oh, sweetheart, I'm not trying to embarrass you. I'm just telling it like it is. Your lips—"

She cleared her throat, hoping to silence whatever he was going to say. "Will never touch yours again if you continue."

Ryan moved to Isabel's table, where she told him some charming story about her dead husband again. She was getting a lot of airplay talking about good ole Henry.

Chloe tried to keep her head down and focused, but it was like being tested on basic skills again with her father there.

She beat the egg whites until they were a perfect consistency and painstakingly folded in the other ingredients. That was the trick to a good soufflé. If you stirred the egg whites, your soufflé would rise, but if you took your time and folded everything together, it was perfection. Once the timer was set and the cheese soufflé was in the oven, she worked on a dark chocolate soufflé. Out of the corner of her eye, she watched Dwayne whip the ingredients together, and she knew as long as her soufflé didn't fall, she wasn't going home.

"Fold, don't whip," she said to Gage.

"Aww, you worried about me hot—"

"Don't say it."

"Over here," Ryan said, moving between Chloe and Gage. "We've got something hotter than a fresh-baked soufflé happening. You mix two bakers, add in a quality show, and toss in a competitive edge, and you've either got a recipe for love or one for disaster. After the last episode's flour play, we're not sure what these two are mixing up." She knew he was attempting to get the home audience members, those old enough to understand what foreplay was, to understand his meaning of flour play. It probably went over most people's heads, but when she looked at her father, she knew he figured out something was going on between Gage and her.

Though Ryan tried to get information from both of them about their "budding romance," they remained tight-lipped except for the little jabs and competitive taunts.

As she expected, Dwayne's dishes fell flat. Isabel beat Gage, but Chloe came out on top with her grandpa Fortney Mason's sinful soufflé.

She was glad she didn't completely flop in front of her father. All her life, all she wanted to do was make him proud.

She wanted him to want her as part of his team. Not because she was his daughter and had a sizable inheritance from her grandparents, but because she was a talented cook who had earned her position in Aspen's elite culinary circles.

They let Dwayne go, and the show wrapped up for the day. They were down to the wire. Three bakers left. The slates were wiped clean, and they were starting from scratch once more. One of them would be named a master baker and given the hundred thousand.

Looking at her father and how he analyzed every move she made, she wanted it to be her. Winning *The Great Bake Off* would be her accomplishment and not tied to her family or the famous restaurants. Chloe could, in her own right, make a name for herself.

Her father walked over with a smile on his face. "Congratulations. I would've expected nothing less than a first-place from you."

For a man so hellbent on first place in everything, she wondered why it was easy for him to make her feel like she'd never been more than a second-class citizen in her family.

"Of course," he continued. There was always an of course. "Your chocolate souffle was a little pale, and you could've gotten more lift if you'd folded the egg whites less."

The excitement she had from her win sunk like a rock in the water.

"Why are you here?"

He looked at Gage, who leaned against a nearby prep table. He appeared ready to push off the table and rescue her at any sign of trouble.

"Is it wise to consort with the enemy? Or was that your plan all along?" He smiled. "Draw him in so he's off his game?" Her father tapped his chin. "You are your father's daughter."

"No, I'm my grandfather's granddaughter." She rocked from foot to foot. Her body was triggered and on high alert. "Why are you here, Dad?"

He sighed. "Isn't it time we doubled down again? You and I

were a talented team, and I miss my right-hand woman. I want you back at La Grande Mason."

She cocked her head and stared. "You want me back?" She played the words she longed to hear over and over again, but they didn't ring true. "As your sous chef?" That had to be it. He probably lost his last chef and needed a replacement. Dad had a reputation for being difficult, but chefs were gluttons for punishment if it meant they could put the Mason brand on their resume.

"No, sweetheart. You'll be in charge. Come home where you belong."

Gage kicked off the counter. "Seriously?" He turned and walked away.

Chapter 18

When Chloe came to the Luxe bakery, Gage had set up for the day's bake. They had cupcakes and quick breads and all sorts of rolls to make. He was halfway to mixing the bread dough when she moved toward the mixer.

"What are you doing?"

"I'm making Kaiser rolls." He added his warm yeast mixture. It was a trick he'd learned from his father that expedited the rising process.

"We don't make our bread here." She pointed to the freezer. "We buy the dough pre-made and just bake it. If the last shift did their job, the rolls would be on the proofing trays ready to go into the oven."

"Sorry, I didn't know." He pointed to the mixer. "What do you want me to do with this?"

She smiled. "Bake it. I'm sure it will be better than what we buy."

He went back to the task at hand and mindlessly did what he'd done for years ... baked. He worked on autopilot while his mind figured out a way to address the issue floating through his thoughts.

He didn't know her all that well, but he liked her and cared about her.

"Can I ask you a question?" She leaned on the table in front of him.

"Yep," he said in a harsh tone.

"Why are you mad at me?"

He ripped balls of dough from the batch and set them on the trays. "I'm not mad at you." He continued to tear the dough into pieces, and by the end of the tray, he was clearly lobbing the dough into place.

"Tell that to the poor dough getting a beat down."

He stopped what he was doing and faced her. "You got exactly what you wanted. He asked you back and gave you everything."

She nodded. "Yes, he did."

"Are you going to take him up on it?"

"We're meeting for dinner tomorrow at the restaurant."

"And you think that's in your best interests?"

"It depends on whether you're speaking professionally or personally." She donned a pair of gloves and started slicing the tops of the dough balls. "It's a boon for my career. I'd be the executive of one of the country's top restaurants."

He nodded because he understood the drive to have something that was his. He'd wanted to take the reins of the bakery for years, and when he could, his hands were still tied by his father's memory.

Chloe was in a similar situation, except her father would be there, breathing down her neck constantly. Her executive chef title would be in name only.

"Do you think he'll actually let you run the restaurant?"

"That's what we'll discuss. Why do you care?"

He took off his gloves and placed his hands on her shoulders. "Because I do. I care a great deal. I want what's best for you."

"I would think you'd be pushing me to take the job knowing how much that means to me."

He pressed his forehead to hers. "I want you to take it if that's what you want but only if it's good for you, and I'm not sure it's good for you."

Over the last few weeks, he'd heard plenty about her father and her family. Her sister Gabby was the sous chef for Mason and McHale's, the restaurant named after her and her boyfriend Flynn. Her mother was mostly absent unless a spa was involved. And her father was a handful. While talented, he wasn't particularly philanthropic with his daughters.

"Maybe he's turned over a new leaf." She scrunched her nose as if the statement smelled foul. "Okay, he probably hasn't, but I want to hear what he has to say. I owe it to myself."

He pressed his lips to hers and stepped back. "As long as you don't think you owe it to him."

"Says the man who still hears his father's voice in his head."

He couldn't argue. Parents influenced everything about you, from how you saw the world to the way you interacted with it. His father had been gone for months, and he still saw him and heard him all the time. That voice told him he owed the family some debt of gratitude for bringing him into this world. He had a very different viewpoint. Children didn't ask to be born, they just were, and when you had a child, it was essential to make sure that you gave them everything they needed to thrive and survive. It didn't mean the things that money could buy, but unconditional love and support—a soft hand to guide when needed and a firm hand when it was necessary. Sadly, his father only knew the firm hand part.

"True, but his voice grows more distant with every passing day, and my voice gets stronger. It's time I stepped out of my comfort zone or the status quo. My family can't expect anything to change if we continue to do the same old thing. I talked to my mother and set the expectations should I win the contest. If I'm not allowed to sell sweets at Sweet Eats, then I can't stay there. There comes the point in your life where you have to take care of yourself. I'm there."

She stared at him for a long moment. "You're right. I have to look out for myself."

"Now you're talking, but ..."—he chuckled—"now that you might leave Luxe and get your heart's desire, you won't need the win as badly."

"Nice try. I can't put the cart before the horse. I don't know anything yet; it's like an interview."

He didn't know her father but knew what the man was thinking. It was the same thing his sister was. What a boon to have a baker who won *The Great Bake Off* on the show. And if Chloe were thinking clearly, she would see her father's machinations at work.

They finished the bread, made the quick bread, and started on the cupcakes.

"Shall we make Adelaide's recipe?" she asked.

"Sure, why not?" From memory, he calculated the ingredients they would need to make them in bulk. "What do you want to fill them with?"

She leaned against the prep table. "Love."

Hours later, after they finished their prep for the day, they gathered their things and walked out of the resort.

"You want to come over?" he asked. "I've got a frozen pizza and a six-pack of beer. I'm sure there's some cheesy chick flick on we can watch while we unwind."

She stared at him, then at her keys like the choice was a hard one to make. "What if I fall asleep?"

"I'll take you to bed." He let his eyes close halfway as he

thought about her between his sheets. "Sassy won't be happy she's been replaced, but she'll get over it."

"Kicking one girl out of your bed to make room for the other seems harsh."

"I only have room in my bed and my heart for one girl at a time. She'll understand."

"All right then." She looked around the garage. "You want to drive, or do you want me to drive?"

"Let's both drive. That way, you can do what you want in the morning and not feel like you have to take me back to my car."

She laughed. "You're certain I'll fall asleep?"

He wrapped his arm around her shoulder. "A man can dream."

Pizza and beer in hand, they sat on his couch with their hips touching. Sassy sat on the coffee table, staring at her competition.

"Are you sure she's okay with the unexpected visit? She's scoping me out in a sinister way. I can see her wondering if she should shank me with her sharp claws or curl into my side and purr."

Sassy leaped from the table to Chloe's side and laid beside her.

"Looks like you made the cut," he said.

"Cut might be the keyword. Maybe she's of the camp that you keep your friends close and your enemies closer." She looked down at the cat. "She looks like a scrapper."

"She's been through a lot. I came home one day, and she walked right in and hasn't left since."

Chloe glanced around his place. "What's not to love. You've got the prerequisite furniture for comfort. There are endless bowls of food and water. You clean her litter regularly, and you pet her when she tolerates it. I'd say this girl is living her dream."

He had to admit that he considered Sassy a lot in his decisions.

He chose a plush couch instead of leather. His carpet was cut pile instead of looped, so she didn't get her nails stuck. He bought a robot vacuum that zipped around his place every day to keep the hair to a bearable level.

"She seems happy." Chloe nuzzled into his side. "You make me happy too."

His heart did a triple backflip and nailed the landing.

"You make me happy, but you know what would make me happier?"

She looked into his eyes. "Winning the competition?"

He laughed. "That would make me happy, but I'd be happier yet if you stayed the night. Not because you fell asleep, but because you wanted to spend it with me. What do you say?"

Chapter 19

It was one thing to fall asleep and not have to take responsibility for that decision, but another to commit to spending the night and all that means. When she was a kid, you never did a sleepover with someone you didn't trust because if you did, you'd wake up with Sharpie markings on your face or your bra soaked in water and then put in the freezer. She'd experienced both, and neither were pleasant. The bra she could deal with, but scrubbing off expletives from her forehead wasn't something she'd soon forget. It took Comet and one of those green, scrubby pads the housekeeper used to clean the frying pans to remove the words that would make her grandma Mavis blush. Not her mom because she'd called her father those words on numerous occasions. Best exfoliation she ever got, and she was only thirteen.

"You want me to spend the night?" She shifted her body to look at him more closely. "What does that entail."

He cupped her cheek. "More kissing, for sure. No pressure at all. It would be nice to have time with you. Time to hold you, and kiss you, and appreciate you."

"By appreciating, do you mean getting naked with me?"

"It just means spending time with you—no nakedness required."

She giggled. "You're asking me for a sleepover."

He kissed her gently. "I am."

"Okay, but no Sharpie on my face and leave my bra alone."

He narrowed his eyes. "Do I even want to know what that means?"

"No, you don't. I'll also need to borrow a T-shirt or something to wear to bed."

"Not a problem."

Light danced in his eyes when he smiled. It was the same look most kids got on Christmas morning when they sat in the living room in front of the tree with a package in their lap, hoping it was everything they wished for. She only hoped he wouldn't be disappointed.

"What side do you sleep on?"

He pulled her into his lap. "I sleep on the side that you don't."

"Who's making breakfast?"

He laughed. "Should I fill out a resume?"

She slugged him lightly in the arm. "I'm simply checking out the amenities."

"I'll make you pancakes."

She threw herself forward and kissed him. "Deal."

They kissed for what seemed like a lifetime. Chloe could spend hours kissing Gage. His lips were like soft pillows of velvet, and no matter what he ate, he tasted like peppermint and passion. They alternated between watching TV and making out like high schoolers, but instead of driving her home and kissing her at the door, he handed her a Silversun Pickups T-shirt and a brand-new toothbrush he got from the dentist at his last cleaning.

She entered his bedroom like a skittish cat and found him lying in bed, reading. Who didn't love a man who read?

"What are you reading?" He showed her a book called *Wheel of Time* before he placed it on the nightstand.

"It's a great series. Kind of a cross between *Game of Thrones* and *Lord of the Rings*." He tossed back the covers for her to enter, and she saw he wore flannel pants and a Strokes T-shirt.

She slid between his soft sheets. "You're on my side of the bed."

He chuckled. "Forgive me." He shifted his body so he hovered over hers on his way to the other side. But she stopped him and pulled him in for a passionate kiss. That kiss led to more—lots more. Before she knew it, they were both naked and in a tangle of limbs, catching their breaths.

"Wow," she said.

"Yes, wow is right." He turned to his side and pulled her back to his chest, and that's how she stayed; in his arms, feeling like she'd won the boyfriend lottery.

Was he her boyfriend? That would have to be ironed out tomorrow over the pancakes he promised.

"Wake up, beautiful."

Chloe opened her eyes to see Gage dressed in his T-shirt and flannel pants sitting on the edge of the bed holding a cup of steaming coffee.

"I put a splash of creamer and three sugars just the way you like it."

She processed that information and smiled. "You were paying attention."

"It's important to know what your woman likes."

She rolled on her side and lifted to take the coffee. "I'm your woman?" She sipped the perfectly brewed cup and hummed. Sore muscles from a wonderfully passionate night followed by coffee in bed delivered by a hot baker were pure nirvana.

"If there is a question after last night, I didn't do my job well enough."

She laughed and nearly spilled her coffee. "If you did any better, I might not be able to walk."

He stood. "I put a towel in the bathroom so you can shower, and I'll be in the kitchen, whipping up the pancakes I promised. If I do that correctly, maybe you'll never want to leave."

She set her coffee on the nightstand and swung her legs over the edge.

"I don't want to leave, but I must. I've got places to go and people to see."

His expression fell. "Your father."

A knot tied her gut, and she suddenly felt nervous. "It will be fine." It was not an attempt to convince him, but her.

"You know what you're doing. I support you."

That knot fell away, and a warm, lovely feeling seeped into her core. Had anyone ever told her they supported her? Sure, she knew her sister did, but they never spoke the words. How nice to hear them.

"I'll shower then." She stood and wrapped her arms around him before lifting on tiptoes for a kiss. "See you in a few minutes."

She stepped back and picked up the coffee, carrying it into the bathroom with her. In the mirror, she saw herself. Not the broken girl needing her father's approval, but the woman who had a man who saw she had value. It was a heady feeling she could get used to.

She pulled back his shower curtain and laughed. Hers was so much better, but she'd give it all up to spend her nights with Gage.

She emerged twenty minutes later to find pancakes and bacon perfectly crisped the way she liked it.

"Are you trying to spoil me?"

He shook his head. "You're a Mason. I'm fairly certain you've lived a spoiled life."

She dropped her fork on the table. "How could you say that?"

He straightened. "I didn't mean it negatively. All I meant was when it came to breakfast, I'm fairly certain you had what you wanted whenever."

It was true. She never wanted for anything but validation and unfettered love. "You can't live on gourmet food and Gucci your entire life." She picked up her napkin and wiped her mouth. "My mother probably thinks so, but she's an apathetic trophy wife. She's the garnish in my father's life, and he's the financier to her monthly colonics."

Gage's face twisted into a picture of distaste. "That's just a waste."

"It seems to work for them. Some people are uninteresting and need others to define them." As soon as she said those words, her heart sunk in her chest. All her life, she promised not to let others define her, and yet she had allowed her father to do just that.

"I think we are all in search of the comfort that validation brings us. It's imperative when it comes to your parents. Do you want my advice?"

She nodded. "Yes. I'd love your perspective since we seem to be fathered by birds of a feather. Hard-charging, never happy, always pushing, parents."

He sat back and picked up his coffee. He sipped it leisurely while she waited for him to find the right words. That was one thing she appreciated about Gage. He never spoke without weighing his words.

"Chances are you'll never get the respect or hear the words you want to hear from him. I hope you do because I know what it's like to want your parent to tell you they are proud of who you've become."

She reached across the table and covered his hand. "I'm sorry you never got that."

He nodded. "Me too, but what it taught me was you have to be proud of your accomplishments. If you can look in the mirror and say you did your best, then that should be enough. I only learned that these past few weeks."

"Who taught you that?"

He picked up a piece of bacon and took a bite, slowly chewing until he'd prepared his answer. "You did, Isabel, Lilly, even your father. I saw him standing there like a giant looming over you, even though he was nowhere near. It brought me back to the days when my father did the same." He took a bite of pancakes, and when he was ready, he continued. "The competition has put things into perspective. At the end of each challenge, I can honestly say that I did my best with the time I had and the given task. There isn't one thing I wouldn't have given my father to try."

"You're a talented baker."

"I agree, but here's the thing. Even my wins wouldn't have been perfect in my father's eyes. Not because he didn't love me but because he didn't know how to love me any other way."

"Will you close the bakery if you lose?"

He pushed his nearly empty plate away. "Yes. There isn't an option. We can't get a loan because the bakery barely sustains itself."

"But what will you do?"

He chuckled. "I'll see if my boss wants to keep me on at Luxe. Then I'll figure out how to help my mother. My sister should be okay. She's a talented accountant and can pick up a few more clients."

"Is that what you want to happen?"

"No, what I want is to turn the bakery into what I know it can be, but that might not be possible. I'm competing against some formidable women. What about you? Will the win give you what you want?"

She thought it would, but maybe he was right. Perhaps the validation she was seeking had to come from somewhere else—herself.

"I don't know."

He tugged her to him and kissed her. "I think the key to happiness is knowing what you want."

She took his hand and led him back to his bed.

"Right now, I want you."

She couldn't believe how late she was running. If she were lucky, she'd make it to La Grande Mason at the top of the hour and not several minutes before, as was expected. She kept telling herself this wasn't about her father but her. But her insides were wrung out from rushing. This was like an interview, but for a job she once had.

The closer she got to the restaurant, the more her doubt filled her. Not that she felt she couldn't do the job. She knew she could. It was Gage's words from that morning that swirled around in her head: *"Even my wins wouldn't have been perfect in my father's eyes. Not because he didn't love me but because he didn't know how to love me any other way."*

Was that what she'd be entering again—an endless cycle of disappointment and regret?

"You're late," her father said as she rushed into the kitchen.

She looked at her phone, and it was five minutes to the hour. "I'm on time."

He grumbled something about never learning and waved for her to follow him. "Let's introduce you to your crew."

"I know my crew. I've been working with some of them all my life."

"As my daughter, but now you'll be their boss."

The thrill of those words danced in her heart. She had to remind herself that this was part of her father's mode of operation. He had you step on the coveted carpet just before he pulled it out from beneath you.

"Gather round," he ordered the kitchen staff. "You all know Chloe. She's competing in *The Great Bake Off*, and if she wins, she'll be your executive chef."

There went the carpet. She tumbled down that hole into despair. "If I win?"

Her father smiled and wrapped his arm around her shoulders, leading her to his office. "Can you imagine what that will do for our brand? We can put that on our advertisements. It's just one more claim to fame that sets us apart from the rest."

She stopped, forcing his arm to drop as he propelled himself forward, almost oblivious to the fact that she was still in the hallway.

"Are you coming?"

She shook her head. "No, Dad. I'm not." She refused to cry in front of her father. To do so would only make her look weaker in his eyes. "You'll have to put some other type of feather in your cap. I'm not your pawn to use as you like. I'm your daughter, and you are supposed to love me."

He turned to face her. "I love you. Now come in the office so we can plan."

She swallowed the lump of sadness in her throat. "Gage was right. You love me in your way but have no clue how to love me the way I need you to."

She turned and walked away, crying all the way to Gage's house. She knocked, and he opened the door.

All he did was nod and pull her into a hug. "You know how to love me."

He kissed the top of her forehead. "If I don't, I'll try to figure it out."

He drew her inside and closed the door. Why couldn't everything in life be this easy?

Chapter 20

Gage was never one to condone violence, but the look on Chloe's face and the hurt in her eyes made him want to kill her father. He wouldn't take a painless approach, either. He considered all the equipment in a kitchen and decided he'd do it with a potato peeler one layer at a time because that's how Michael Mason destroyed his family. Every criticism or false high he gave chipped away at the layers of Chloe's self-confidence.

After he calmed her down, he held her for hours until she said she needed to go home to change. He was certain she was there, crying her eyes out again. Since they were off from the show and the bakery, he said he'd bring over her favorite Chinese food, and they'd stay at her house. There was no way he would spend a night without her now that he knew what his life was like with her.

He parked in front of La Grande Mason and spent five minutes in his car, deciding if confronting her father was worth it, and he decided anything that protected Chloe from hurt had to be.

He walked into the nearly empty restaurant because five o'clock was too early for most diners who enjoyed that caliber of restaurant.

"Welcome to La Grande Mason," the host said. "Do you have a reservation?"

He shook his head. "I'm here to see Michael Mason."

"Do you have an appointment?"

"I don't need one. I have a complaint."

"Oh," she said, looking around her like she was checking to see if anyone heard. "I'll be right back."

She hurried away and came back with Chloe's frowning father. "Oh," he said. "It's you. Did my daughter send you?"

Gage shook his head. "No, she doesn't even know I'm here."

Michael chuckled. "Never let your right hand know what your left hand is doing. I operate like that too."

"That's not it at all. I just came to tell you a story."

Michael looked at his watch. It was an expensive one with all the mechanics showing through the glass.

"I don't have time for a story."

Gage nodded toward the closest table. "You don't have time to miss this one." He didn't wait for Michael to agree; he took a seat and a breath.

"My father was a lot like you—driven by something I'll never understand. He got up early and went to work each day. He came home and ate and fell asleep on the lounger. My mom used to tease and say she married a farting, snoring La-Z-Boy. That was his life. He did it seven days a week without fail. The only other pleasure he got was making sure his kids knew they would never be good enough to make him proud, and you know what ... we never were." He let that sit for a moment before continuing. "He died in that chair one night. He just took a deep breath and let out his final exhale. My dad was born miserable and died miserably."

Michael stared at him. "And why did I need to hear this story?"

"Because there's still time for you. Part of being a good human is caring for others in a way they can't for themselves. Sometimes it requires muscle. Other times it's money. The most important form of care comes from the heart, and you still have time to find yours."

He didn't wait for Chloe's father to respond but got up and walked out the door.

"How much Chinese food did you get?" she asked. "This must have cost a fortune."

"You said you like that paper-wrapped chicken and the sweet and sour pork. I figured if I got enough, we wouldn't have to worry about making lunch or dinner since we have work and the show tomorrow."

He'd been thinking a lot about the show, and while he desperately needed the money to save the bakery, the bakery did not define him. When it came to Chloe, her accomplishments did. She was a driven individual who had been raised to succeed. And every failure was a rusty blade to her heart.

"Let me pay for dinner. What do I owe you?"

"Nothing." He laid out the food on the island, pushing the *Recipes for Love* book to the side. "I can afford to buy my girlfriend dinner."

"Girlfriend?" She opened the paper-wrapped chicken and took a bite. "I like the sound of that." She pulled the little bite of teriyaki chicken from the paper and popped it into her mouth. He loved the way she ate. He could enjoy the food without ever tasting it. All he had to do was watch her savor it. "Will you still be my boyfriend if I beat you on *The Great Bake Off*?"

He dished up a plate of orange chicken and rice. "I can separate the show from the person. Can you?"

He cocked his head and waited for her reply.

"I've always been an all-in type of girl." She sat on the stool next to him.

"Does that mean all in the relationship we're starting or all in the competition?"

She turned to face him. "Can't it mean both?"

"Sure. I just know that the competitive edge can sometimes skew priorities."

She pulled her knees to her chest, sitting on the stool like a bird perched on a wire.

"Are you telling me that if we're dating, you're not putting your best foot forward?"

He shook his head. "No, that's not what I'm saying at all." He wasn't telling her that, but how did he explain how he'd learned since his father died that relationships were far more valuable than a win? He wished he'd had a closer relationship with his father. He wished he'd been able to break through the tough outer shell to see if there was a softer side. He wished he'd had the chance to prove himself worthy. Then again, he wished his father had seen value in him as a person outside of the bakery. That was where his family went wrong. They were more than bakers. Some individuals had lives outside of baking bread.

"Then, what's the problem?"

"There is none. I was just thinking about our situations and how similar they are. We both need validation."

"I'll never get it from my father."

He knew that story. "Probably not." Did he tell her he went to see her father?

As he opened his mouth to confess, her phone rang.

She picked it up from the island counter and rolled her eyes. "Speak of the devil."

He blurted, "Wait," but it was too late. She let the call go through.

"Hello, father," she said with little emotion in her voice.

He watched the knots form in her shoulders and tighten her into a mass of tension.

"What?" her voice squeaked. "He what?" She stared at him.

He'd seen that look before on his sister's face when she wasn't sure if she wanted to hug him or slug him.

"I didn't send him." Her eyes narrowed. "No, I haven't changed my mind." She hung up and frowned. "You visited my father?"

"Yes. I should've asked, but it was an impulse decision."

"Why would you do that?"

"Because I care about you, and I don't want you to feel unvalued."

She snorted. "Oh, I know my value, and it's tied directly to the bottom line. If I can't pull my weight, then I'm not wanted."

His shoulders sagged. "I didn't mean to overstep my boundaries, but I wanted your father to know how amazing you are."

The hard crease between her furrowed brows relaxed. "You think I'm amazing?"

He reached down and grabbed the leg of the stool and dragged her closer. "I think you're like Adelaide Phelps's buttercream frosting."

"That good, huh?"

"Better."

"What did you tell my father?" She inched to the edge of the stool to get closer.

"I told him a story. We never talked about you specifically."

She picked up a cheese-filled wonton. "What was the story?" She took a bite.

He told her the gist of what he said to her father. "Basically, without coming out and saying it, I insinuated he could make different choices which would improve his life."

"And you did that for me?" She fell forward and pressed her head to his chest. "No one has done that for me."

He wasn't about to get slugged, but instead, hugged. Pleasing

Chloe was like sprouting wings. It made him feel like he could soar to any heights.

"Someone should've been in your corner all along."

She brushed her lips against his. "Yours too."

They stuffed themselves and cleaned up before heading to the couch. Gage snapped up the cookbook and brought it with him.

"Tell me about this cookbook. Is it a family thing that's been passed down?" He flipped through the pages of the handwritten recipes.

"No, that's the thing, it just showed up in my locker one day."

"Like appeared out of thin air?"

She nodded. "Seriously, I opened my locker, and there it was. Either the universe wanted me to see it, or someone in the restaurant is playing Cupid."

"Why Cupid? Because it's called *Recipes for Love*?"

She reached over and turned the book to the preface. "Read it."

He did and smiled. "Do you think this book has magical qualities?"

She laughed. "I don't believe it's magical, but there is something magical and romantic about the notion of a recipe bringing you love."

Gage flipped through the pages. "Forever Fudge Cake, Savor Me Strudel, Lure Me Ladyfingers? Maybe we should make Sensuous Spice Cake."

She grabbed the book. "No, you're only allowed to make one recipe, and I made the Kiss Me Cupcakes."

"Do you believe that if you made a second recipe, your chance at love would evaporate?"

She pressed her lips into a thin line, and a crease settled between her brows. "I'm not one to tempt fate. Lately, without bad luck, I might not have any at all."

"It's all perspective." He set the book aside. "Neither one of us wanted to be in this competition, but if we weren't, we wouldn't be sitting here together. Is that bad or good?"

"Good, definitely good."

"Right, so the bad was the competition, but in truth, it was good. There always seems to be a balance—a yin and yang of sorts."

"Which is good? The yin or the yang?"

He turned his head and kissed her forehead. "It depends on how you're looking at it."

"Okay, I get it—perspective." She wrapped her hands around his arm and laid her head on his shoulder. "But you won't hate me if I win, will you?"

Chapter 21

Chloe stood at her workstation, waiting for Ryan to announce the challenge. That left only three of them—her, Gage, and Isabel.

"Today, we're spicing things up a bit," he said. "We've put together a box of ingredients that the contestants need to use in their cupcakes." He moved the length of the floor and stood in front of Gage's prep table. "Before, the contestants could pick and choose their ingredients, but now that we're down to the wire, this contest needs to compare apples to apples, so the first ingredient is... Yep, you guessed it. Apples. Open your boxes, bakers, and get to work. You've got forty-five minutes to come up with an award-winning recipe for a delectable cupcake. The tally from the next two days will determine who's the greatest baker."

The lids went flying as the three contestants dug into their baskets. Inside, she found apples, cayenne pepper, and kumquats.

"Tangy, fruity, hot it is," she said.

Going straight for the food processor, she pulverized the apple into apple sauce. It was a brilliant move to incorporate the apple to add moisture and flavor.

Then she mixed the ingredients, using Adelaide Phelps's recipe for the basic cupcake. It was probably the best batter recipe she'd ever had—definitely award-winning. As usual, her prep table was a dust storm of flour and sugar. Not that she liked to work messy; she simply got so involved that she didn't pay close enough attention.

Looking at Gage's space, she almost felt guilty for her mess. Not guilty enough to do anything about it just yet, though—she had work to do. She preheated the oven and scooped the batter into paper muffin cups, and as soon as the preheat buzzer rang, she popped the tray inside and went to the pantry to get additional ingredients. She didn't want to showcase the cayenne but thought a kumquat, orange, and apple filling might be nice. She could add in a smidge of the pepper to give it a kick, but she'd stay away from using it as a key ingredient.

A look at Isabel showed the woman to be calm and working through her process methodically. She was also making an apple pie filling, but not like her.

"Bakers, you have thirty minutes."

For the next twenty minutes, Isabel tried to psych Chloe and Gage out by telling a story of her great-grandma's recipe and how many blue ribbons it won.

Gage shook his head. He mixed his ingredients and made his buttercream frosting. She watched as he added the exact ingredients of Adelaide Phelps's recipe.

"You didn't." It wasn't a statement but more of a shock.

"Didn't what?"

"Use Adelaide's recipe."

He took in a silent but chest-filling breath. "I did. It's the best I've had."

She stood and stared at him. Her insides were aflame with rage. He'd spent a long time last night looking through that book, no doubt stealing recipes. "That's not yours."

"It's not yours either." He let out a growl. "It's a recipe book, Chloe. It's public domain."

She stomped her foot. "No, it's one of a kind, and it belongs to me." Her face had to be red because her cheeks burned like she'd taken a torch to them.

"It's temporary ownership. You read her rules, and it said bake one recipe and one only, and then you'll be tasked with passing the book on to another."

Ryan and the cameraman were taking in the argument that would become prime-time drama for the audience. She hated that this was happening, but watching Gage use her recipe made her feel sick to her stomach.

Her old feelings of being betrayed bubbled up, and bile rose to burn her throat. She ignored the camera in her face and let her insecurities direct the conversation.

"Did you get close to me just to get my recipes?"

His head fell back, and he laughed.

She couldn't believe he was amused at her expense while the show gobbled up the drama with closeups.

"Yes, that's right. I went after you and seduced you just to get close enough in case you had an award-winning recipe in your possession. Are you listening to yourself?"

She had to admit that it sounded ridiculous.

"Did you say seduce?" Ryan asked.

She mixed her apples and oranges and put them on the stovetop to boil down to a sweet filling.

"I'm not talking about my love life to you."

She went back to her station and cleaned it up. America already thought she was a mess, but she didn't have to be messy. She wondered when she let her life get so out of control.

Gage walked over and whispered in her ear. "Can we talk about this later?"

She sighed. "Maybe." She knew herself. If he won the chal-

A Dollop of Delight

lenge using what she considered her recipe, she wouldn't talk to him again. That wouldn't be much different from stealing another's ingredient so they couldn't compete fairly. To her, it was a monumental betrayal.

Her cupcakes came out of the oven fluffy and perfect. Moments later, Gage's and Isabel's came out looking just as lovely.

At this point, it was anyone's game, but she wanted it to be her game. She needed this win.

She hollowed out the centers of her cupcakes and set them aside while she squeezed the juice of the sour kumquats into her filling.

She was genuinely ridiculous, and she knew it, but she couldn't help herself. There was always someone coming in at the eleventh hour and stealing her win away. Typically, it was her father, but this time it was Gage.

She filled her cupcakes and thought about what Adelaide Phelps said. The batter was basic. Chloe imagined the woman wasn't only talking about baked goods but people in general. It wasn't the outer shell that always made them special, but what was inside. As she thought about Gage, she considered who he was on the inside. On the outside, he looked good enough to eat. He was a perfect cupcake with fancy frosting. On the inside, he was like the ingredients in the basket. He was as sweet as a ripe apple, sometimes tart like a kumquat, and oh so hot when it came to everything else. Why was she so angry he used the recipe?

He was right. It was a recipe that anyone could use if they had it, but somewhere deep inside, she felt like it was only hers for a while.

She made her buttercream frosting and added the zest of the kumquat to the mix. When she plated up her cupcakes, she was confident they were winners.

Off to her right, Isabel was adding special touches like silver-coated candies and gold sprinkles. Chloe didn't need the accouterments. Her cupcakes would speak for themselves.

To her left, she watched Gage plate his cupcakes. If she didn't know better, she would've said he'd stolen her cupcakes because they were identical. *He stole the recipe.* She tried to quiet her inner bitch and took a few Zen breaths to calm her agitated self. She let her mind run through the days leading up to today—meeting Gage and the fun they had. Then it drifted to her father and the reason he wanted her back. The heat of anger rose up her spine like an out-of-control fire. By the time her focus was back, the judges had tasted all three cupcakes and declared Gage the winner.

She was blazing inside and knew Gage didn't deserve her wrath. She was mad at life, not necessarily at him, but knowing who she was and how she would respond to the loss, he would take the brunt of her rage, so she smiled for the camera, and when the director said it was a wrap, she didn't say a word to anyone. She turned and walked away.

"Chloe, wait up." Gage ran after her, but she just couldn't talk to him.

"I've got nothing to say."

He rushed ahead and stood like an impenetrable wall. "Are you really mad that I used that recipe?"

Was she? She heaved a sigh. "No, I'm mad that you used my recipe and beat me."

"Oh, come on. You heard what the judges said."

She shook her head. She hadn't heard a thing. "No, I didn't. I zoned out."

He placed his hands on her shoulders. "They said they couldn't decide whose cupcake they liked better. They were both award-winning, but they chose mine because I integrated the cayenne pepper and made it a standout ingredient."

"I came in second?"

He inched closer. "No, baby, in my book, you'll always be first."

She leaned into him. "Thanks, but in a baking contest, that won't matter."

He kissed her lips. "Maybe not, but in life, it will. We won't be in the contest forever. Tomorrow's our last day, but life ... we're here until we aren't."

She wrapped her arms around his waist. "Why do you like me?"

"I don't," he said matter-of-factly.

She snapped back to look at his smiling face. "You don't like me?"

"No." He shook his head. "I'm falling in love with you."

"You are?" Her heart melted like warm chocolate. The sweetness rushed through her veins.

"Unequivocally."

"You're a crazy man, Gage Sweet."

"Crazy for you." He stepped to her side and wrapped his arm around her shoulders. "Shall we go downstairs and make more quick bread? You know, the recipe you stole from me to use for the resort."

"Hey," she reprimanded. "You said once the recipe was made, I could use it." She knew he was making a point, and she agreed. "My anger wasn't at you." She felt ashamed for even insinuating he'd hooked up with her to steal her recipe. "I was being ridiculous. I was revisiting that meeting with my dad. He only wanted me back because he thought I had a chance at winning."

"You do. Out of the three of us, you're the most talented. The problem is, you're so focused on the win that you can't see how wonderful you are. You want your father's validation? You just got it. He knows you can win, and he tried to get you to come back to the dark side so he could take ownership of your wins. You don't need him to believe in you. Believe in yourself."

He was right. What would the win mean to her? In the end, it meant very little. All her life, she'd been searching for validation, and even when she was sure she'd get it, there was always something that wasn't right, or perfect, or up to Dad's standard.

"You're right. I have to be happy with me."

"Do you think you can be happy?"

"You make me happy." She smiled up at him. He was such a handsome man with a gentle soul. To think his father never saw his value was heartbreaking. At that thought, she realized that somewhere between the first day they met and now, Gage had become stronger.

"What happened to you? Where is the man who came into this contest still trying to prove something to his father?"

"I realized there are more important things than attaboys. Life isn't about my accomplishments. It's about my contributions. Do I want to win? Yes, I do, but will my life end if I don't? No. Will a win bring back my father? No. What a win will do is provide for me, my mother, and my sister, but we'll survive if I lose."

"But you'll probably win."

She was almost certain he would. On some level, she hoped he did. He had far more riding on the line. Isabel was using the money to take her family on a cruise. A win for Chloe was about stroking her ego. An ego that got a boost today with Gage's wise council. He was right. Everything was about perspective. It wasn't about her accomplishment either; it was about her contributions. Her biggest question now was how could she give back to the man who had given her so much? Gage made her feel like she was capable of anything. He made her believe she could scale mountains and sprout wings to fly. Love was powerful, and she had to confess that she was falling in love with him, too.

She remembered her Grandma Mavis once telling her that love is defined not by what you get but by how much love makes you want to give. At that moment, she was ready to give Gage everything.

He tugged her closer to his body as they walked out of the conference room door. Off to the side, Isabel talked to the same guy as before. He worked for the production company, and she was always around him, smiling, laughing, and talking.

"You think she's a cougar?" Chloe asked.

Gage chuckled. "She's something, alright."

Chapter 22

Gage didn't know why he was so nervous. Maybe it was because his sister had called three times in the last hour, making sure he was in the right headspace. His mother called twice, wishing him luck and telling him she was wearing her four-leaf-clover necklace, hoping to bring more to him.

Last night, Chloe stayed at her place and he at his. It was the first night they'd spent apart, and he didn't like it, but he understood why she needed it. They rarely got sleep when they were in bed together.

They were the perfect ingredients when mixed. Both a little sweet and a little bitter, and that rounded them out.

He considered the *Recipes for Love* cookbook. He wasn't much into superstition, but it was the cupcakes that ultimately brought them together... and the flour fight that caused him to strip naked and need a shower.

While the recipe itself could tear them apart, it didn't. He knew Chloe could've gone either way when he used the recipe, but he made a point and risked it all to prove something to himself and her.

A Dollop of Delight

It was a recipe that didn't become all that special until you decided what would go in it. He had plenty of time to read through the cookbook and Adelaide Phelps's stories, which were far more delectable than what they created. Reading the book was like having your grandmother in the kitchen with you, teaching you how to be a good person. He wanted to try out so many of the recipes but wasn't one to test fate. The rules said one recipe and one only, and the book wasn't even his.

He fed Sassy and gave her a scratch under her chin. "Wish me luck." He knew he didn't need luck. In the end, life was pretty simple. You never needed more than enough, and for him, Chloe was enough.

They lined up in the center of the kitchen and listened while Ryan outlined what would happen that day. The challenge was to bake a cake, but the kicker was that it had to be top-tier wedding cake worthy. The panel would judge them on presentation and taste.

"We have to make a wedding cake?" Isabel asked. "I've made the wedding cakes for my children and grandchildren."

Gage ignored her. The one thing he learned about Isabel was that her superpower was intimidation. She hid behind her cameo-wearing grandmother persona, but inside she was a red-hot little devil. Too bad he hadn't seen this side of her before he brought the sabotage to the producer's and director's attention. Deep in his gut, he thought she was the culprit. It was too coincidental that disasters befell those closest in proximity to her. He had the ingredient mix-up. Matt was gone because he was too basic, but that came after a fall. The floor was slick, but no one could say if that was from the batter or something more sinister like a coat of baking spray. Then there was Lilly, whose oven was not calibrated or turned up. Dwayne seemed to flush out on his own. The only one who didn't have a disaster was Chloe, but Isabel pointed the finger at her initially, and he trusted the older woman. What grandma would be blatantly dishonest? She presented her case in the guise of helping him.

"Then this should be a shoo-in for you," Chloe said. She leaned in to whisper to him. "Kick her ass. I'm tired of her trying to psyche us out."

Since this was the last day of taping and they weren't filming yet, he pulled Chloe to him and gave her a soft, sensual kiss.

"No matter what happens today, remember that we are a team outside this competition. Adelaide Phelps said it's what you add that matters, and having you in my life is the secret ingredient to my happiness." "Aww, you are so sweet, but I'm still going to beat you." She pressed her lips quickly to his one more time. "Then I'm going to love you." She winked. "You know, really love you ... a long time ... in bed."

His heart took off racing. "I see what you're doing. You're trying to knock me off my game."

She giggled. "I knocked you off your game weeks ago."

He rocked his head back and forth. "True, but now you're playing dirty."

"Is it working?"

His clothes suddenly felt too tight and the lights above too hot.

"We're on in five, four, three…"

Ryan explained the rules, and they had three hours to complete their masterpieces. It was a long time compared to their usual forty minutes to an hour, but this had to look pretty and taste great.

"We have enough time to grab a coffee," he teased. "You want one?"

Chloe gathered her baking supplies. "I'll pass, and you should, too."

"If you're going to win, you'll need to bring your A-game."

"If *you* want to win, you'll bring *your* A+ game. I've got this. Don't forget, I work at a resort where weddings happen all the time."

He loved the banter they had while they prepared their ingredients.

He carefully measured the flour. "But have you made a wedding cake?"

She blushed beautifully. "No, but I made a Chantilly cake my boss said was amazing."

He listened to the judges talk about Chantilly cakes and how tricky working with the fruit could be.

"Is that what you're making now?"

She made a pfft sound and rolled her eyes. "Like I'd tell. Get your cake in the oven, and I might divulge."

He whipped up a simple cake batter. It was perfect for his plan. He stuck the three layers in the oven and went to work on the filling and buttercream icing. He wasn't much of a cake decorator but he was reasonably certain he could do as well as Isabel, who seemed to shop in the pantry more than she was baking. She came back with a bag full of decorations like edible silver and gold leaves.

"Where were those?"

She smiled. "In the pantry. You just have to know where to look."

Using premade would save her a lot of time, and since they were uniform, her cake would probably come out looking perfect. While he would like to have the money, the win wasn't all that important, whereas the victory was essential to Chloe. As long as Isabel didn't win, he didn't care who did. He had a job—one he liked, working with Chloe. In the end, that was enough. He'd figure out what to do about his mom and the bakery. The sale of the building could give her a nice little nest egg, provided it wasn't hocked to the hills.

Ryan moved to each of them and asked what the win would mean. He started with Chloe, but she didn't look at the camera or Ryan. Instead, she turned and stared at him.

"The win is the smallest victory of the competition."

"What do you mean? A hundred thousand dollars are riding on this cake."

"True, but there's a lot more riding on it as well." She wiped her hands on a nearby towel. "I've learned that baking is like life. There are the rises and the falls. Where there is sweetness, there is bitterness. It's not the result that truly matters. It's the journey and the ingredients you mix to get you there.I started this contest not even wanting to be involved, but sometimes we don't have choices, and we have to take what we're given and make something wonderful from it."

"Tell me what you gained from this experience?"

She smiled and looked into Gage's eyes. "Perspective."

Ryan nodded and moved toward Gage. "What about you? What will a win mean to you?" He stood silent for a moment and pondered the question, but mostly Chloe's answer. "I feel like I already won." He moved from his table and walked toward Chloe. "I fell in love. How can you put a price on that? Would I give her up for a hundred thousand dollars? No way. She's a million-dollar find."

"So, it *is* a love match."

"I'm the cake, and she's the frosting. She's the cookies, and I'm milk. We are both fine on our own but infinitely better together."

Ryan turned to the camera. "That right there is a true recipe for love."

He moved to Isabel. "Same question for you."

She touched the cameo at her neck. "A win for me is a win for my whole family. It's been ages since we all got together. That cruise would reunite my family." She pointed to Chloe and Gage.

"Imagine that kind of love but multiply it by ten. A win will bring this old lady joy and happiness."

Gage wanted to hate her love spiel, but he couldn't. Everyone deserved a little happiness, and a hundred grand was hard to pass up.

The buzzers went off on all three ovens simultaneously, and they dashed to pull the cakes out. He glanced left and right and saw that all of them looked perfect.

He went into the day with a plan, and as long as everyone did their part, even if they didn't know what their part was, it would turn out fabulous.

As the time ticked down, he created a basic cake. He didn't do anything fancy. It was plain and simple and part of the plan.

He peeked over at Chloe and saw her making a whipped topping rather than an icing. "That's a mistake," he said. She was making her famous Chantilly cake, but instead of an icing that would stand up to the heat of the lights, she was making a whipped frosting that was sure to melt.

"No, it's not. I know what I'm doing." Right then, he knew she was doing what he was, and that was throwing the competition so he could win.

He stared at the clock and saw she didn't have time to start over again. "Don't do it. I did the same, and you know what that means, right?"

Her mouth dropped open, and she leaned over to see Isabel placing her premade leaves and petals.

"We're in trouble."

"Yes, we are." He pushed his cake to the side and rushed to her. "What can I do?"

She glanced at the clock. "Nothing. There isn't time." She needed to wait until the last minute before she iced the cake. Then she stood a better chance of winning if it didn't slide off right away.

As the seconds wound down, she tacked layers of fruit on the top. It was a beautiful cake, but it wasn't a wedding cake.

He inched back to his table and stared at his creation. It was more suited for the end of something rather than the beginning.

They both stared at Isabel's masterpiece. It looked like it belonged on the top of three tiers. All it was missing was the porcelain bride and groom.

"Times up, bakers," Ryan said. "Who do you think will win the hundred thousand dollars?"

They stood in the center as the judges tasted and critiqued their cakes.

Philipe Pierre started with Gage. In his oh so French accent, he said the cake was basic. The only saving grace was the apricot filling, which paired nicely with the icing. "As for decoration, there's nothing to write home about."

His heart sunk to his stomach. He knew losing would feel bad, but he thought he was doing it for the greater good. He was giving Chloe what no one in her life ever did—a chance at validation.

"Chloe," Gretchen McGraw started. "Your cake is fabulous. I love the custard and the fruit but the frosting." She moved what looked like a puddle of cream on her plate. "It wasn't a wise choice."

"I understand," Chloe answered.

He could hear the hitch in her voice and moved closer so he could hold her hand. "It's okay."

"What did we do?"

He smiled at her. "We gave everything up for love."

The judges had positive things to say about Isabel's cake. They thought the icing was nice but didn't like it as much as Gage's cake. The cake itself was moist but wasn't as good as Chloe's. What they liked were the decorations. It was the only cake that looked fit for a wedding.

A Dollop of Delight

Most dramatically, Ryan said they would break and would be back in a few minutes to award the winner the prize.

As soon as they went to break, Isabel rushed over to the man she'd been friendly with. They had a brief conversation before he picked her up and swung her around. Her laugh was so loud that no one could miss it.

"Love blooming again on the set?" Ryan asked while the makeup artist powdered his shine.

"Of course not. Toby is far too young for me. Besides, he's my—"

"Fan, I'm a fan." He gave Isabel a stare that could make a soldier quake. No one missed the exchange.

Hildy moved forward and grabbed the guy from production. "Back to your places."

Ryan did the countdown, and they rushed back to their spots before the camera turned to them. After several minutes, they announced Isabel as the winner.

Chloe was the first to shake her hand and congratulate her. As soon as he walked toward her, Hildy ran onto the set, waving her clipboard.

"Stop," she said. "She can't win."

Everyone on the set went silent. "What's going on here."

All eyes went to Isabel, who minutes before floated on cloud nine, but now sunk like a popped balloon.

Hildy pointed to cameraman two. "Stephen has evidence that Isabel broke the terms of her contract."

Everyone gathered around the camera as he played back the footage from minutes before. "I didn't stop the filming because sometimes what I get when no one is paying attention is great for the outtakes. What I didn't expect to find was evidence that Isabel and Toby are related."

"But we aren't. I'm not her kin by blood," Toby said.

They all watched Toby pick up Isabel and swing her around.

He called her Gran and said something about how fun the cruise will be.

Hildy shook her head. "No, but maybe by marriage."

Knowing they were seconds away from finding out the truth, Isabel yelled, "He's my grandson-in-law."

"You knowingly broke the rules," Hildy said.

Chloe stared at Isabel for a minute. "Oh, my goodness. Not only did you try to get me booted for allegedly sabotaging the contest, but you had someone on the inside." She turned and faced Gage. "It was Isabel who switched the baking soda with cornstarch."

Isabel shook her head. "No, it wasn't me. It was—"

"Don't say it," Toby said.

"But you did it."

"Because you told me to."

Isabel stomped her foot. "I didn't tell you to reset the temp on the ovens."

Toby shoved his hands in his pockets and shuffled nervously back and forth. "No, but you had me plant the leaves and petals."

Hildy screeched. "I knew those weren't available in our pantry."

The director yelled cut even though no one was filming. "We have a huge problem here."

Ryan laughed. "What we have are ratings. Never has a baking show included sabotage, romance, and sweet treats."

The contestants were dismissed for an hour while the staff determined how to solve the dilemma. Isabel and Toby were asked to stay behind.

When Gage and Chloe returned, it was decided they would broadcast what they had but unveil the treachery to boost ratings. They revisited the tapes and determined the other contestants lost on their own merit or lack of it. Matt delivered basic muffins. Lilly's lemon basil mint bread was a miss. Dwayne left when he considered a praline a cookie. That was right after his theater popcorn concoction was a definite miss.

The producer asked Chloe and Gage to take their places.

"Are we filming again?"

Leo nodded. "We don't have a budget to extend our time on location. Since neither of you was the standout winner, we're going to have a quick-fire round.

Gage's mind raced to what they would have to bake.

"And we're back." He pointed to Chloe and Gage. "Who knew there could be so much treachery in the kitchen? In an attempt to right the wrongs, we are having a face-off between Chloe Mason and Gage Sweet." He stared into the camera. "You know what I love?"

He waited as if the audience was saying, "What, Ryan?"

"I'm in the mood for a brownie." He spun to face them. "You've got an hour, and your time starts now."

"An hour?" Chloe complained. "It takes forty minutes to bake."

Ryan laughed. "I'd suggest you get started."

There was no time to waste. He and Chloe raced to get ingredients after preheating their ovens. In the pantry, they stood side by side, swiping similar items from the shelf.

"Play to win," Chloe said. "If I beat you, it's because I'm the better baker."

He knew he had to give it his best shot. By throwing the contest last round, both of them lost.

"Same rules. No matter what, we put us first."

"Agreed." She nodded and raced back to her table, tossing ingredients into the whirring mixer.

Usually, neat as a pin, Gage didn't have time to line up his components. All he could do was follow Chloe's lead and bake like his life depended on it.

He wasn't sure what brownies he'd make but knew they had to be amazing if he was going to win.

His best option was to toss in everything, so he dumped in nuts and chocolate chunks along with bits of brittle he found on the shelf.

He glanced at Chloe, who placed her brownie batter in the oven.

"Plain brownies?" he asked.

"Not on your life." She smiled while unwrapping caramels and tossing them in a pan. She was a genius.

"Turtle brownies?"

"Maybe."

He poured his batter into a pan and placed it in the oven. "How are you going to spend your hundred grand?"

She laughed. "Oh, I have a plan."

He'd taken the easy route, so he had little to do while she bustled around the kitchen, heating caramel and toasting pecans. When forty minutes passed, Chloe pulled her brownies from the oven and put them directly into the cooler. She tapped her foot nervously. "Come on ... cool down." She kept looking at the clock.

His timer went off, and he pulled the brownies from the oven. They were perfect. He had a little trick up his sleeve, too. He whipped up a chocolate bourbon sauce and drizzled it over the top. As soon as he was sure it soaked into the brownie, he cut them into three-by-three squares and plated the treats up and garnished with a swipe of melted chocolate and a dollop of delight with real whipped topping.

Next to him, Chloe worked feverishly, slicing her brownies in half and filling them with caramel and toasted pecans. When she was finished, she dripped a string of caramel across the top and placed a single perfect pecan on each.

When the time was up, there was nothing either of them left

behind. They brought their best to the competition and whoever won deserved it.

As the judges devoured their brownies, he and Chloe stood side by side, holding hands. No matter what the outcome, they both came out on top.

Phillipe asked for another brownie from each of them. "I must have this recipe ... both." He kissed his fingers and thrust them in the air. "Perfect."

"I agree," Gretchen said. "However, one stands out a little more than the other." She leaned into Phillipe and whispered. He nodded. "While we love them both, the winner is ..."

Chapter 23

ONE MONTH LATER

In honor of *The Great Bake Off,* Chloe and Gage made their brownies for the watch party that Allie set up in the conference room where the show was filmed.

It wasn't easy keeping the secret, but everyone was bound by the contractual obligation not to divulge the winner or the order of elimination until the show's finale.

Gage remained working at Luxe, and Chloe worked right beside him. They made an excellent team.

"Tell me," Gabby leaned into Chloe and whispered.

She shook her head. "I can't, and I won't."

"I'm assuming you didn't win. Otherwise, I'd be able to see it in your eyes."

"Or maybe I'm getting better at hiding my emotions."

Her sister laughed. "Girl, that's so not true. I've been watching you watch him all night. You're in love."

Chloe glanced at Gage, who was deep in conversation with Julian. She was in love with him and wasn't hiding it.

"I'm not hiding my love for him, but I won't divulge the details of the show."

"You're a brat."

"So, you've said since I can remember."

The door to the conference room opened, and the light flooded inside. A back-lit shadow of a figure moved forward. Chloe would recognize him anywhere, even from an outline.

"What's Dad doing here?"

"Oh, I invited him."

Chloe sucked in a breath. "Why would you do that?"

"Because he's trying to turn over a new leaf. He said he had an epiphany one day and decided if he didn't change his ways, he'd die alone and lonely."

Chloe was taken aback because that was exactly what Gage had told him. At that moment, she loved him even more.

"Chloe ... Gabby, how are my girls?"

Gabby lifted on tiptoes and kissed her father's cheek. "Oh, you know, living the dream."

He turned toward her. "Clo, tell me, did you win?"

She laughed. "If I did, are you giving me La Grande Mason?"

He wrapped his arm around her shoulder. "Nope, I think it's best to separate work from family." He kissed the top of her head. "In trying to create something great, I ruined what I already had, which was pretty damn wonderful." He glanced between both girls. "I'm sorry."

This was what waking up with amnesia must be like. She didn't know this man at all. This stranger in front of her was who she wanted as a father, not who she'd gotten. Could someone do a complete turnaround? Usually, that required a life-altering event.

She looked over her shoulder at Gage, who had a watchful eye on her father. She knew if her dad so much as stepped out of line, he would be there to defend her.

"It doesn't matter if you won or lost. I'm just so proud you tried."

Allie tapped a microphone. "Can I have everyone's attention?" She waved for those in the room to come closer.

Chloe looked around as the off-duty staff gathered at the front of the room.

"Mason and McHale's has graciously provided dinner for everyone." She pointed to the side table where warming trays kept the food warm. "And Gage and Chloe have kindly made something that I'm told shows up in this last round. Enjoy and let's see if there's a winner among us."

There was no mention of Isabel, who would play a huge part in the last episode, and no one seemed to notice she was missing.

The lights dimmed, and people milled around, getting plates of food, and taking seats as the show started.

She and Gage sat beside each other and watched the show as if it were new to them.

"Chloe better keep that Gage guy," he said.

"Oh, she's definitely keeping him."

"Are you sure you're happy with the plan?"

She turned to face him. "I've never been surer of anything in my life." A life with Gage seemed like a no-brainer. They were one of those couples who knew what the other thought without a word being said.

While the show played, they sat and stared into each other's eyes. She never would tire of him. Like the cupcakes that brought them together, his eyes contained something special. It wasn't the gold and black specks that seemed to sparkle like precious metal and polished onyx when he smiled. No, it was the love that filled them when he looked at her.

A gasp came from someone in the room, and her attention went to the big screen.

Another voice whispered, "I knew she was crooked. It's always the sweet ones you need to watch."

Gage chuckled. "It's the grandmothers who know how to bamboozle."

Heads turned toward him. Allie stopped the show after Ryan announced the tiebreaker. "Go grab a brownie, and we'll do our Luxe taste test and vote."

Moments later, when everyone sat eating chocolaty goodness, she started the show again. And just before the winner was announced, she hit pause and took a vote.

"Raise your hand for the Turtle Brownie." She counted and smiled. "Now, all in favor of the Bourbon Brownie."

They chose Gage's creation. Chloe turned to him and smiled. "You made the better brownie."

He kissed her lips. "There's no accounting for taste. Besides, I'm pretty sure most of the staff here are day drinkers. It's the only way to put up with the guests."

Allie called them to the front. "So, who do we think won? Who did the judges pick?" They stood off to the side while she pressed play, and Chloe was announced the winner of *The Great Bake Off*.

Friends and family and workmates rushed them both with congratulations and condolences. They shook hands and hugged everyone like they were in the receiving line of a wedding. At the end of the line was her father.

"I'm so proud of you." He turned to Gage. "You better treat her right, or you'll have me to answer to."

Gage lifted his brow. "You better treat her right, or you're answering to me."

Her father patted Gage on the back. "We'll hold each other accountable." He leaned in and kissed her cheek. "That one is a keeper." She held Gage's arm and rested her head on his shoulder. "I agree."

Allie was the last person to approach them. She smiled and

sighed. "I'm so proud of you both." She gave them both a hug. "Now tell me, when do I have to have your replacements?"

Although it was a conversation they needed to have, she wasn't expecting it now.

"How did you know we are both leaving?"

A broad smile brightened Allie's face. "If you saw what everyone else did, you'd know that there's no way you two aren't going into business together." She looked around and then whispered as if a thousand ears were tuned in when only a few people remained. "If you weren't heading in that direction, I would've pushed you. Some people are workers, and others are leaders. You're the latter and need to create, and that will require freedom. The only way to be free is to be in charge of your own destiny. All I need is for you to check a few resumes for me. Maybe sit in on a couple of interviews."

Chloe looked at Gage. "We can do that, can't we?"

He nodded. "Anything you want, babe."

Allie laughed. "That right there is a smart man. You know the saying, 'Happy wife, happy life.'"

Chloe shook her head. "We're not there yet."

Gage wrapped his arm around her waist. "But we're close."

She spun to look at him.

"We are?" She didn't know what he had up his sleeve or the secret he was keeping close to his vest, but there was something he wasn't telling her. There was a lot of whispering at Sunday dinner at his mother's. Even his nephew couldn't keep the snickers at bay.

"You ready to go home?"

She nodded. "Yep, Sassy won't be happy if we keep her waiting too long."

"Sassy?" Allie asked.

"She's our fur-baby."

"That's how it starts. You cohabitate. Once you share the friends and animals, singledom is over."

"And coupledom begins. And you have to stay together because it's too hard to decide who gets to keep the pets and the people," Allie said.

Gage chuckled. "Sassy was my cat, but she likes Chloe better."

As if telling a secret, Chloe leaned in but spoke in a normal voice. "It's because I sneak her extra treats."

"Tell me, was it the show that brought you together?"

They both shook their heads, but Gage was the one who spoke. "We met once before the show but were thrust together because of it. What brought us together was a flour fight."

"The one we saw on air?"

Chloe felt the heat of a blush on her cheeks. "No, we were following this crazy recipe book, and I got an urge to have a food fight, but flour was what I had."

"And after that, I showered, she stared, and we baked cupcakes. If you peel back the layers, it was the cupcakes that brought us together. They were aptly named Kiss Me Cupcakes, and I kissed her like my life depended on it all night."

Allie narrowed her eyes. "*Recipes for Love?*"

They both gawked at her.

"Do you know the book?" Chloe asked.

Allie turned and walked away. "No," she said innocently. As she moved toward the door, she called over her shoulder. "It's probably time to pass it on."

Chapter 24

ONE MONTH LATER

He led Chloe blindfolded down the street. Today was the re-grand opening of the bakery. She'd generously donated her winnings to help with the restorations. She said she was never in it for the money. In the end, they were the perfect match. She needed the validation, and he needed the cash. Together they got what they wanted. Long gone was the drab white of the bakery walls, and in their place were soft tones of pink, brown, and green. It was like a delectable garden had sprouted.

"Why do I have to be blindfolded? I saw the bakery yesterday."

He shuffled her forward. "I know, but the sign is up."

"I've seen that too. It says Sweet Eats."

"Maybe." He didn't let her know their new beginning would start from the ground up. "Are you ready?"

She danced around. "Yes, I'm ready."

He placed her where she'd get the best view and pulled the blindfold off.

"Dollop of Delight—a C and G Sweets bakery."

"Aww, that's so sweet. You used your sister's and your initials."

He turned her to face him. "No, silly." His hands cupped her cheeks. "It's Chloe and Gage Sweet. Do you like it?"

She looked up at the sign, and tears sprang to her eyes.

"Do I like the idea of you and me?"

"Well, yes, that, but also, the name?"

"But I'm not a Sweet."

He grinned. "Not yet, but I'm banking that you will say yes someday." He'd asked her a dozen times, but she wasn't one to rush into anything. "Don't make me return that new stand mixer I got you as a promise gift."

"Oh, my goodness, you got me the Hobart?"

Any other woman would want a diamond but not his girl. She swooned over a mixer.

"I did."

She threw herself into his arms. "If you decide to ask again, let's say in about a month or two, I'll probably say yes."

"Probably?"

She giggled. "Okay, definitely, but only because I don't want you to have to change the sign, which is amazing."

They entered the bakery to find his mother behind the counter. "Welcome to Dollop of Delight. I'm sorry I have little to offer because our bakers have been outside staring at the sign."

Gage lowered his head. "Sorry, Mom. We're on it."

His sister rushed out of the office. "I've got to run, but I left the new ledgers on the desk."

"Where are you off to so early?"

She frowned. "I've joined an early riser exercise group."

"That's awesome."

"It's fine. I'm willing to subject my body to endless amounts of torture if it gives me a chance to meet other adults. I see you two and ..." She shook her head. "I want some of what you have. Is there a recipe for that?"

They looked at each other and laughed. "There might be."

"Whip me up a batch of true love, will you?" She started for the door. "Jesse is in the office. Mom's taking him to school today. I'll come by later for my bag."

Courtney, dressed in yoga pants and tennis shoes, dashed out of the bakery.

Gage turned to Chloe. "Are you thinking what I'm thinking?" She spent the greater part of the night looking at the note left for her in the back of the book. When she opened it, she laughed and told him she knew exactly who'd passed on the book to her.

The note read, *Never judge a book by its cover or a dessert by its baker. Some things are better than they appear.* She took out a piece of paper and wrote something to the next recipient. Because the book was given to her, he wasn't privy to the message, but he knew it would be good.

"Did she say her bag was in the office?"

The book is leaving the resort. If you want to read more *Recipes for Love* Novels, get A Layer of Love

A sneak peek at A Layer of Love

"A recipe for love?" Courtney Sweet pushed the cookbook across the kitchen island. She had no idea where it came from. All she knew was it somehow found its way into her backpack.

If only it were that easy and there was a recipe. She'd make a fortune selling it.

She laughed all the way to her early riser's exercise group. This was her first meeting, and she hoped to make a few friends and talk about something other than action figures and anime.

Her son Jesse was entertaining, but nothing took the place of a bonafide friend. As for love ... that left the day Marcus did. She said three words that made him run. "Hey, I'm pregnant." That was almost eleven years ago, and she'd been single ever since.

Seeing her brother find happiness with Chloe only made her realize how much she needed the company of others. Why not add people with fitness? If it all worked out the way she hoped, she'd gain a few friends and lose a few pounds. Win-win.

She pulled into the parking lot of Pioneer Park, where several people in various athletic outfits milled about. It was an Aspen crowd dressed in designer duds who looked more like they were walking the runway than the nearby trail.

Courtney stared at her baggy, paint-splotched sweats, and the sneakers she hadn't worn in at least a year. She wasn't Aspen chic but Timberline real. She didn't get her hair cut in salons called Posh, but in front of her bathroom mirror with scissors dulled by her son's school projects.

She gave the crowd another glance and almost started her car to drive away, but a man hanging off to the side caught her attention. He wore baggy sweats like hers and a vintage Queen T-shirt. At least he had good taste in music.

She got out of her beat-up Jeep and made her way toward him, but it appeared the housewives of 81611 had the same idea and swooped in like crow attacking roadkill.

They lobbed questions at him like they were tossing hand grenades, and he avoided their interrogation like a professional, landmine sweeper.

"Good morning," the group leader said in a high-pitched voice. She could have been an advertisement for Lululemon in her multicolored ensemble. "This is a walking group that meets Monday, Wednesday, and Friday at this location. We'll do the four-mile path today. If you need a more intensive workout, consider adding weights." The woman bounced in place like she'd had one too many espressos. "Hopefully, you got to introduce yourselves, but if not, there's plenty of time during the trek. Shall we go?"

She led the way down the paved path. No one followed her initially. Courtney thought they were all waiting for the hot Omega man to go ahead of them. When he didn't budge, his fan-club trio walked on.

Once they were on the trail, Mr. Handsome followed. Maybe he was an ass man and liked the back-end view of things.

As she fell into line behind him, she appreciated the scenery he offered. Though his sweats were baggy, they draped like a beautiful fondant frosting across his backside.

For that first mile, she hung back and took in the sites. The mountains and forest were lovely too.

Reminding herself that she joined the group to meet people, she double-timed her pace to catch up to him.

"Hey, how's it going?" she asked as she came upon his right.

He gave her a cursory glance followed by a frown. "Fine."

She laughed. "You know, when a woman says fine, it's anything but."

His scowl deepened, creating a deep furrow between his brows. He picked up his pace as if to escape her.

She resorted to a wog, which was a half walk and half jog to keep up with him.

"Well, obviously, you're sight-impaired or gender challenged because I'm not a woman. I'm a man, and when we say fine, it's generally the truth."

"Fine."

He cocked his head and stared. "Is that anything but fine?"

She didn't know what his problem was. All she tried to be was friendly. "It's you're an idiot fine."

He narrowed his eyes and seemed to lurch forward. When she looked down, she noticed his shoe was untied.

"You want me to teach you how to double knot?" she asked.

"Now, who's being a jerk?"

Her six-year-old inner child was fighting to be freed. All she wanted to do was stick her tongue out and possibly her foot to see him face plant on the pavement, but she reeled her unhappy woman-child in. "You're right. I apologize." The words had a bitter tang to them. It was fine to say sorry when she was in the wrong, but this guy was out of line.

"Look, I get it. You show up and think, I'll give the only guy in the group a go, but honestly, I'm not interested."

She nearly tripped over her shoes, and they were tied. Double knotted, in fact.

"You think I was trying to pick you up? Listen, dude, you're not my type."

He stopped and tied his shoe, and like an idiot, she waited for him. That was part of her problem. She was too accommodating ... well, she used to be, but that was nearly eleven years ago. Now she was simply afraid of putting herself out there. And just her luck, the first guy she strikes up a conversation with is a total troglodyte.

"Oh, you have a type?"

Her blood heated, and the pressure inside her built until her scalp itched. Having a conversation with this man was like sparring with a toad, warts, and all.

"Yes, I prefer them human with a smidge of decency, an ounce of kindness, and a spoonful of humility. What you are is a pound of pain in my ass."

"That's quite a recipe you've got going there. If I had to build one for myself, I'd want an hour of silence and a mile of space. If you added in a cool breeze, I'd be golden."

She snapped her fingers. "Wish granted." She marched a few feet ahead and took up residence between the group of women she'd never fit in with and the man who she never wanted to see again.

Fifteen minutes later, a phone rang, and she turned to see the guy stop to answer it. He let out a few expletives and left the group, jogging toward where they started.

The women in front talked about Dysport and Sculptra and who in town gave the best colonic. Courtney wondered how she'd gracefully bow out. Could she fake a turned ankle and hobble back to her car?

Her phone rang, and she breathed a sigh of relief when she stopped to answer it, and no one waited for her.

"Hello."

"Ms. Sweet. This is Abby, the nurse at Pine Elementary School."

Courtney's heart thundered in her chest. The nurse only called when something was wrong.

"Is Jesse okay?"

She picked up her pace until she was jogging to her car.

"Yes, he's fine, but Principal Cain asked me to call. She'd like you to come in. There was an event involving Jesse, and your presence is required."

What the hell was an event?

"Do I need to bring him a change of clothes?" The only thing she could come up with was an "accident," and Jesse hadn't wet his pants since he was three. There was the time Gage pinned him down and tickled him when he was six, but in her son's defense, he literally had nowhere else to go when his uncle wouldn't let him loose.

"No." She paused for a moment. "It's not that. Are you on your way?"

"He's not hurt?"

"No, but he's in trouble. There was a fight of sorts."

She swallowed and let the thought nearly choke her. Jesse wasn't the kind of kid who got into trouble.

"I'm on my way." She hung up and ran the rest of the way to her SUV. Whatever happened, there had to be a logical excuse.

Like a bat flying straight out of hell, she raced to the school and parked illegally in the staff parking lot. She opened the door and tried to exit, but the seatbelt choked her, so she sat back and took a few breaths. A calm, cool, and collected parent would take a moment to regroup and gain her bearings, but she was already wound up by Mr. Mean.

She yanked and tugged herself free and stomped toward the front office. Jesse Sweet was exactly as his name described. He was sweet and kind and considerate. If there was a fight, he was the victim.

At the front office, she waited for the woman behind the desk to notice her. When she didn't, Courtney cleared her throat and tapped her nails on the counter to gain her attention.

The gray-haired woman looked up and pushed back the glasses perched precariously on the tip of her nose.

"Can I help you?"

"Sweet."

The older woman smiled. "Only on Mondays. By Friday, I'm an out-and-out ogre."

Courtney let out a frustrated sigh. "No, I'm Courtney Sweet, and I've been summoned here about my son, Jesse."

"Right." The woman whose nameplate read Mrs. Wheatley shook her head. "Principal Cain is waiting for you." She pointed down the hallway. "Last door. Knock before entering."

Courtney traveled the long corridor like she was walking the green mile. Each step that she grew closer to the door, the more her panic set in.

She'd always heard that being sent to the principal's office was like being sent to the firing squad, but she considered that the opinion of a ten-year-old in trouble. Everything was a life-or-death matter at that age, but she truly felt like she was approaching her demise.

Was it because Jesse was in trouble, and this might be the end of the sweet boy she knew and loved, and the start of him being a pre-teen? She shuddered to think about what that meant.

At the door, she raised her hand and let it fall to her side twice before she got the courage to follow through and knock. A shudder passed through her. What would be waiting when the principal told her to come inside.

She tapped the door four times. Four was always her lucky number, and she hoped it would hold.

A Dollop of Delight

"Come in," the firm voice called from the other side.

She gripped the handle and pushed the heavy door open.

Her jaw dropped when she saw who was waiting on the other side.

"You've got to be kidding me," Mr. Mean said.

Sitting beside him was a toothless little girl with brown curls and swollen lips.

On the other side of the room was an unhappy-looking but seemingly unscathed Jesse.

At her throne was Principal Cain.

All four of them stared at her.

Nope, four was no longer her lucky number.

Dear Baker

Dear Baker,

Adelaide Phelps' cookbook will leave the resort, which seems fitting since recipes should never be hoarded but shared.

When I created the cookbook idea for this series, I thought of my grandmother who was a Phelps, but her name was Isabel. Everything she made was simple, but because it was made with love, it always tasted better.

Fill your life with flavor. Fill your world with love.

Kelly

Kiss Me Cupcakes

Before you begin, wash those hands because you don't want the surprise ingredient to be E. coli.

Ingredients:

1 1/3 cups (185 grams/6.5 ounces) all-purpose flour

1 teaspoon baking powder

1/4 teaspoon salt

1/2 cup (1 stick/115 grams) butter, softened (No margarine or lard here.)

1 cup (200 grams/7 ounces) granulated sugar

2 large eggs at room temperature (If you have a chicken coop, just grab a few from under that chicken's butt.)

1 teaspoon vanilla extract (Use the good stuff because quality counts.)

1/2 cup (120 ml) whole milk

Instructions:

Preheat oven to 350F/180C. Line muffin tin with cupcake liners and set aside.

In a medium bowl, sift together flour, baking powder, and salt and set aside.

Beat together butter and sugar until light and fluffy. Then add in the eggs, one at a time, mixing well after each addition. Add in the vanilla extract and beat until combined. Next, add half of the dry ingredients and mix. Add in the milk and beat until absorbed. Add the other half of the dry ingredients and fold until the batter is smooth. Do not over-mix—the less you mix, the lighter the cake will be.

Feel free to customize your cupcake by adding chocolate chips or fruit bits or jam. As long as you don't change the liquid-to-flour ratio, you should be fine. Cupcakes are a lot like people; they can be filled with all kinds of magic. Maybe your cupcake isn't the vanilla version. If that's the case, look a little harder and dig a little deeper for the surprises inside.

Once the batter is ready, divide it evenly between the cups, filling them about 3/4 full. Bake for 15-20 minutes or until a toothpick inserted into the center comes out clean. Allow cupcakes to sit for 10 minutes, then remove from the pan and allow to cool completely on a wire rack. Frost with my favorite buttercream icing.

Phelps Famous Buttercream Frosting:
Ingredients:

1 cup (225 g/2 sticks) unsalted butter, softened to room temperature

1/8 teaspoon salt

4 cups (480 g) powdered sugar, sifted, plus more as needed

3 tablespoons heavy cream

2 teaspoons pure vanilla extract

1 teaspoon freshly squeezed lemon juice

Instructions:

In the bowl, beat butter and salt until smooth and creamy, then add 2 cups powdered sugar and mix until combined. Add another

2 cups and beat until completely smooth. Add cream, vanilla, and lemon juice and beat until fluffy. Incorporate more sugar as needed until desired consistency.

Like the cupcakes, the frosting can be full of surprises, too, by adding ingredients like fruit jam, lemon curd, orange zest, chocolate, and more.

Other Books by Kelly Collins

Recipes for Love

A Taste of Temptation

A Pinch of Passion

A Dash of Desire

A Cup of Compassion

A Dollop of Delight

A Layer of Love

Recipe for Love Collection 1-3

Recipe for Love Collection 4-6

The Second Chance Series

Set Free

Set Aside

Set in Stone

Set Up

Set on You

The Second Chance Series Box Set

Get a free book.

Go to www.authorkellycollins.com

About the Author

International bestselling author of more than thirty novels, Kelly Collins writes with the intention of keeping love alive. Always a romantic, she blends real-life events with her vivid imagination to create characters and stories that lovers of contemporary romance, new adult, and romantic suspense will return to again and again.

For More Information
www.authorkellycollins.com
kelly@authorkellycollins.com

Printed in Great Britain
by Amazon